# In Fields Where Love Grows

## Rachel Anne Jones

IN FIELDS WHERE LOVE GROWS
Copyright © 2024 by Rachel Anne Jones

ISBN: 979-8-88653-334-7

Published by Satin Romance
An Imprint of Melange Books, LLC
White Bear Lake, MN 55110
www.satinromance.com

Published in the United States of America.

Cover Design by Caroline Andrus

*I dedicate this to Douglas, always.*

*And to my friends and family for all their love and support.*

*I dedicate this to the enjoyable visit I had with the client who shared with me the details of a crop assessor, which was my inspiration for this story.*

*Thank you, Nancy, for believing in this story and to Caroline and Ashley for your killer covers.*

*"Some old-fashioned things like fresh air and sunshine are hard to beat."*

LAURA INGALLS WILDER

# ONE
# BRIDGET

THE LAST THING I need to see this early in the morning is Thomas Butros standing in my wheat field scratching his head. While this particular pose is nothing new for my elderly neighbor who can't keep his big beak out of my business, I'd rather he do it on his side of the fence.

I glance in my rearview mirror at the dusty Beamer that was all sparkly and new just minutes ago before the state inspector started trailing me. I resist the urge to punch the gas. I shouldn't have let him follow me so close. My nosy neighbor has the worst timing. I don't need Thomas and his trouble-making self butting into my business or laying a gnarled, crooked finger on my crops in the middle of an inspection.

The tires of my trusty Forerunner crunch on the gravel as I come to a screeching halt. I jump out of my green machine and try not to look as worried and hurried as I feel as I jog over to see what all the fuss is about.

"Well, I'll be danged," Thomas says as I come up behind him. He may be kind of old, but he is no small man. He stands with his feet spread apart and a meaty hand on each hip. I peek around one side of him.

"What is it?" I stand on tiptoe near his right side where his good ear is.

He points at something grunting and rolling around on the ground. "What you got there is a wild boar. I do believe it's dyin'." He takes off his hat and wipes his forehead with the back of his hand. "The darn thing was staggerin' around in circles right before it tipped over on its side."

I watch in horror as the ugly creature's legs kick air. It takes one last grunty ragged breath.

Thomas looks down at me. His crow's feet crinkle a little extra as his gaze focuses on me. "Bridget, it looks like you've got one dead pig on your hands."

Rocks moving beneath the man's feet draw our attention towards the road. We both turn to watch the suit step out of his dust-covered Beamer and proceed to walk down the steep embankment leading to the deep ditch. His shiny shoes almost slip out from under him.

I fight to hide a smile at the thought of him getting a grass stain or a mud spot on that snazzy three-piece suit of his. He dresses fancier than any crop appraiser I ever saw. The sight of his dirty Beamer makes as much sense as his shiny rims that rolled up my driveway first thing this morning, interrupting my cup of coffee.

"Sure is a shame that shiny black car of his has a fair amount of dust coverin' on that fancy, citified paint job," Thomas murmurs, or at least he thinks he does. I never can tell if he realizes how loud he talks, or if he has officially reached the age of free wisdom and not giving a darn who hears it.

I can't help but giggle. "Yeah, it's a real tragedy."

Thomas chuckles. I can't believe I'm conversing in a civil tone with my only neighbor for at least ten miles. We've been feuding for almost a year, but my beef isn't really with Thomas. It's with his son, Tommy Junior, who's as creepy-crawly as the various and sundry of wildlife he's been hauling into my wheat fields on a regular basis over the past month-

and-a-half. My lack of sleep is making me awful cranky, which must be the only reason why I didn't take the time to give the suit a proper introduction. He asked me if I was Bridget Bell before flashing me the nicest smile I've ever seen at the foot of my front porch steps.

I told Mr. Hollywood and his trooper shades to follow me before promptly hopping in my Toyota and leaving him in the dust.

Mr. Fancy pants with his pearly whites stands in front of me and Thomas. His hand is out. "Hi, I'm Trevor Bennett," he says to Thomas. "You must be her father."

Thomas and I look at each other. An unspoken word passes between us. I manage to tell Thomas to hide the pig with me. I step a little closer to Thomas and make the most of my sixty-one inches as I clear my throat. Thomas glances nervously behind us. He's not very good at my unspoken game. "This man is not my dad," I say.

Trevor looks confused. "Oh? Then who is he?" His pointed tone suggests that he is more concerned about my personal affairs than a crop assessor should be.

"I'm her neighbor," Thomas supplies.

"What are you doing in her field?" Trevor looks like he's about to whip out a notebook.

I shrug as if it's perfectly natural for Thomas to be standing where he is without my permission. "He just told you. He's my neighbor," I ground out from between clenched teeth. Trevor is nosier than necessary. This will not bode well for me. "Occasionally he checks on things to be sure everything is going as it should be."

"And is it?"

"Yes! Go ahead and have a look. You'll find my wheat stalks are plenty healthy and growing at a rate that clearly demonstrates sustainability." I point in every direction other than behind me.

Trevor shoulders his solid form between us and almost

3

knocks me over. "I'd say assessing a crop's hardiness and vitality is my job, not yours." His comment sets all my nerve endings on fire. I cannot believe the gall of this man, which would irritate me further if I wasn't so on edge. It must be the second layer of socks I forced myself into before jamming my feet into boots that pinch my toes that has me feeling all jangly. It can't be Mister smarty-pants know-it-all, even if he does make that suit look awfully good. "I wouldn't say it's going all that great, ma'am."

My toes curl inside my rubber boots that my overalls are tucked into. I feel a bit ridiculous in my dad's long-sleeved flannel, but I hate bugs even if I am a farmer. I'm also resisting the fact that I'm destined to be a dedicated Iowa farmgirl despite the proof staring me straight in the face.

Trying to hide a dead, diseased boar from a state inspector is not the best idea but I don't have a new one yet. I think I feel a panic attack coming on. This is the first time it's happened since I've moved back home and it is not welcome. I close my eyes and pinch the skin between my eyebrows as I try to think of what to do or how to escape to my happy place. I don't care which one comes first, so long as I can stop thinking about Trevor, aka Hottie Inspector, finding a dead pig in the middle of my field just months from harvest.

Visions of a brown-haired girl with her long, flowing colorful skirts wearing her ever-present stylish sunglasses, sitting beside a big white fluffy dog at a little round table beneath the awning in between customers enjoying the fresh air bring a smile to my face. The three years I've been away from my beloved Boston suburb fall away. The niche I carved on the corner of third and Jones is long gone, but it remains a piece of my heart. I can still see the friendly welcoming faces inscribed on the glass window of *Banjo's Books and Molly's Pots* on the opposite side of the street.

A throat clearing takes me back into the present.

"My name is Bridget." I'm certain he already knows it. I don't know why he's calling me ma'am other than to annoy me. If the inspector's done his job, he's read over my file. I'd bet almost anything Arnold briefed Trevor on his future clients before he retired. Arnold was nothing if not thorough. I was glad I followed my instincts with Arnold when I had him over for pie the first time we met.

Arnold was a super nice guy for an inspector who worked for the state, so long as you stayed on his good side. I think we got on so well because he reminded me of my father.

There's something about Trevor that makes me want to keep him at arm's length.

He chews on a piece of wheat stalk as he stares down at the dead animal. "You've got yourself a dead boar with the case of glanders."

I stare at the offending pig. "Glanders. Isn't that like a disease in third-world countries with no clean water?" I feel a bit judgy and mean, but I'm desperate. The last thing I need on my hands is a sick pig. It's bad enough trying to imagine where this stupid animal came from, although I don't wonder that long before an idea comes to me. I have a pretty good idea Tommy Jr. knows, but I'm not ready to give my pesky neighbor up to the suit. I don't know Trevor well enough, but I know Tommy. There's a big difference between stupidity and malicious intent.

"I'm not sure it's not glanders. There are many other conditions that can present in the same way. Aren't you being a bit presumptive?"

His chiseled jaw tightens in the corner of my eye. *Chiseled? Really? Why did that word pop into my head? I've gotta stop reading romance novels to fill up my empty love life.* Great. I've pissed off the crop inspector and he hasn't even started checking out my stalks. This isn't the best way to start. "My dad was the Chief Epidemiologist for the *entire* state of Iowa

5

for many years. I think I know what glanders looks like. And that pig is deader than a doornail."

His outdated idiom tugs at my heart unexpectedly. I can't believe my eyes are watering over a phrase just because it brings my grandfather to mind. It sounds exactly like something he would say.

I duck my head to wipe my eyes and will my throat to stop tightening. I get a hold of myself before raising my head to look at my reflection in his obnoxious Oakley's. "There's no question the pig is dead. Have you ever seen glanders firsthand?" I eye the dead boar from the side. I almost wish the bothersome pig would get up off the ground and start snorting. I move my foot in the direction of its hoof.

"I wouldn't touch that pig if I were you. The mortality rate of a human with glanders is pretty high. It's not something you want to fool around with."

I throw my head back. "Stop saying that word. You don't even know if that's what's going on."

He makes a noise that's somewhere between a groan and a growl. It ties my stomach in knots. This is absurd. "It may not be, but until it's ruled out the responsible thing to do would be to handle that boar with proper PPE."

My eyes bug at his pompous manner. "Excuse me?"

"Personal protective equipment," he says in a loud slow voice. "Gloves, mask, and a gown. It's best not to risk exposing any part of yourself to any part of that pig in transport."

It's not wise of me to poke at him, but I can't take his know-it-all demeanor. "Actually, you would need more than just ordinary PPE. If it was glanders, and I'm not saying that it is, you would need double gloves and a well-fitting mask. Once bacteria is in the air, it can enter any exposed orifice. All it needs is a little breeze to go airborne."

I glance over at Thomas Butros, who watches the road.

How is it my neighbor can't hear me speaking loudly in his face but he can hear truck tires coming from a mile away? I turn to see nosy Sheriff Sam Walsh barreling down my road in his brand-new truck. I stifle a groan. My morning just went from sucky to suckier.

## TWO
# TREVOR

I SHOULD PROBABLY TAKE off my shades. That would be the polite thing to do, but something about this petite brown-haired, hazel-eyed lady who looks more like a teenage girl in her overalls standing beside me has me all sorts of fired up. First, she tries to hide a dead animal from me, and now she's telling me the thing isn't diseased. I can't tell if it's because she really doesn't believe me or if it's because she doesn't want this inspection to go wrong.

Either way, it already has. The level of professionalism that should exist between us has gone completely out the window, but she's the one who started it. I don't know what bee got in her bonnet, but it feels like it started the moment she saw me coming up her driveway. I've never had a female be so rude to me. I don't think I like it, just like I don't like her and the old farmer standing off to the side being all hush hush.

"That's all we need. A bunch of humdingers from the city stickin' their moronic noses in where they don't belong," the old farmer grumbles. I try to keep my jaw from dropping at his insult. Doesn't he realize I can hear everything he's saying, or does he not care? The man can't be that oblivious even if he is hearing-impaired, judging by the volume of his words.

"What's goin' on Bridget?" the Sheriff calls from the road. I hate that I'm jealous over his familiarity with her. I can't help but notice the way her ponytail swishes back and forth as she strides towards him as he starts down the side of the ditch.

"Sam." She doesn't sound too excited to see him either. Good. Maybe it's not just me she's annoyed with.

"We've got a body!" the old farmer hollers from somewhere off to the side. I don't like following this farmgirl around like a lost puppy, but I don't want to miss what's said between her and the Sheriff, whose face just got a whole lot less friendly.

"You've got a body," the Sheriff repeats.

Bridget swats at his lower arm. "Relax, Sheriff. It's just a dead pig."

Sam exhales and slows his step. "That's a relief. If that's all it is, I'll just get back to making the rounds."

I clear my throat. "That's not all it is. The boar has glanders." I feel foolish trying to sound more important than I am, but I can't seem to stop.

I meet Bridget's hazel-eyed glare. Part of me knows I'm hiding behind my sunglasses, but the sun is awfully bright today. "The boar *allegedly* has glanders," Bridget corrects me. "There's no evidence that proves it one way or the other. At this point it's all suspect."

The Sheriff says nothing. Bridget and I stop glaring at each other long enough to look over at him. He's on his phone. "It says here glanders hasn't been in the United States for forty years. Do you think this is an act of agroterrorism?"

The old farmer behind me sounds like he's choking. What's that about? "I'm sure there's no act of terrorism going on, Sheriff. If anything, it's probably just a practical joke gone too far," Thomas suggests once he recovers from his coughing fit.

Bridget's hazel eyes narrow in his direction. "What do you know about this pig, Thomas?"

"Nothing."

The Sheriff turns his back to us. His head tilts down and to the left. I hear static. "We're going to need to shut down all roads leading out of the county. Put a hold on transporting any livestock or animals of any kind. Send out an email from the extension office to the necessary FFA members." There's static again. "Yeah, call an emergency meeting tonight. We're gonna need to reroute the bicycle race. I know it's tomorrow. We'll need to set up some detour signs. No one's coming down Bridget's road. There's been an incident. Possible widespread contamination. Could be airborne. Livestock in origin. All facts aren't known yet. No need to panic. Just call a meeting. We will work it out as it unfolds. No, no. We'll worry about that later during the hotwash. Copy that."

Bridget rushes him from behind. Her finger taps on his shoulder at the speed of a woodpecker. He swats at her finger before turning back around.

"Sheriff, stay off that two-way radio of yours before I toss it beneath my Forerunner tire and smash it to pieces," Bridget demands. I almost laugh. I can't believe she's talking like that to the law.

Sam gets a sheepish look on his face. One hand covers his two-way radio as if he actually believes she's going to rip it off his uniform. "Now Bridget, there's no need to set your hair on fire. I'm just taking the necessary precautions. It's my job."

She crosses her arms and stares him down. "Is it? 'Cause it feels like it's your job to spread my news all over town like it's cow manure."

It may be my imagination, but I think his neck just got a little darker. "Are you accusing me of being a gossip? I supplied the proper persons with the basic information they need to know."

"You didn't need to say it was in my field!"

"He didn't," I counter. I'm pretty sure that's going to get me in hot water with her.

"I can speak for myself," the Sheriff says as he looks over at

11

me. I toss up my hands and take a few exaggerated steps backwards. The Sheriff gives me a nod. "You'll be happy to know Kelsi is coming over shortly from the extension office to move that dead boar." He keeps one hand on the butt of his firearm.

Bridget snorts beside me. "There's no need for that. I'll move the dang thing myself. This is my field and my problem." She looks over at Thomas. "You wanna give me a hand?"

He looks at me, the Sheriff, and then back at Bridget. "I didn't bring any gloves."

"Oh, for Pete's sake, don't any of you have any imagination at all?" She stomps up the hill towards her Forerunner.

The three of us watch her out of curiosity as she stops beside the vehicle and whips open the door. She leans over the seat.

"I've got a Kevlar vest in the truck!" the Sheriff yells through cupped hands at her backside sticking up in the air as she leans over the seat. "Is that considered PPE?" he yells again before looking over at me with a smirk on his face.

Bridget shoves off the seat and stands up before whipping around to stare us down from the road. "I'm sorry, Sheriff, but I don't find you funny. If you don't want to help me, just say so!"

The Sheriff shrugs before turning to face me. "In what capacity are you here?"

"Are you asking *me*?"

He grins. "Yes. I know Thomas pretty well so I'm not really wondering what he's doing here. These two feuding farmers keep my drives on this side of the county quite frequent."

Thomas has moved his position up to the corner of my eye. He kicks at the dirt. "We aren't feuding."

"I wouldn't exactly say you're getting along," the Sheriff replies.

"He's a crop inspector," Thomas says as he points in my general direction.

"Aha," the Sheriff says before looking back at Thomas. "I can't help but wonder at the strange timing of a dead boar being found in her fields on the day of the inspection. Do you think that's more than just a coincidence?" Thomas just shrugs.

Bridget walks clean around us. She drags a big piece of cardboard behind her. "Thomas. Do you have a hankie I can borrow?" She unwinds a piece of barbed wire fencing that's wrapped around an old post.

"You really oughta have a pair of gloves on for that," the Sheriff warns. "You don't want to stab yourself on a piece of old baling wire. Then you'll need a tetanus shot."

She levels us all with a sweeping look. "Guess it's a good thing Jamie's down at the health department, isn't it. I'd rather she poke me with a needle than any of you. Now if you'll excuse me, I'm going to prepare this piece of cardboard for transporting a dead boar." She takes the blue hankie from Tom's hands.

"What about gloves for your hands?" I don't know why I'm asking her anything. She clearly doesn't need any of our help.

She points to a couple of transparent corners sticking out of her front overall pockets. "They're called sandwich bags, boys. Improvise." She folds the hankie into a square and straps it to her face with two tan-colored newspaper rubber bands that cut into her cheeks. She then squeezes her face into a pair of child-sized goggles. Her hands stumble around the top pocket of her overalls, feeling for the sandwich bags but I'm not about to help her. The last thing I need to be doing is touching the front of a hostile female. Somehow she wrangles her baggie-covered hands into another set of sandwich bags.

We all watch in horror and fascination as she somehow manages to drag the dead boar onto the cardboard. I hear a few grunts and groans before it's all the way on there. Satisfied, she grabs a hold of the baling wire and starts tugging.

13

The cardboard doesn't move. There's a ripping sound and the wire remains in her hand, but the cardboard and the dead pig haven't moved an inch. Bridget tosses the wire in my direction before grabbing a hold of two corners of the cardboard with her sandwich-bagged hands.

By the way her eyes bug from behind her goggles, I'd say anger is the only thing that keeps the cardboard from sliding out of her bagged hands as she drags the dead boar over the dirt and across the grass. No one says a word as she takes the long way to get to the flattest part of the field before going up the slight slope that leads to the gravel road where her Forerunner is parked.

"She's the most stubborn woman I've ever met," the Sheriff mutters. I couldn't agree more.

"Yep," Thomas Butros says as he nods. "That's what would make her a perfect match for my son. He needs someone who can keep him in line."

The Sheriff harrumphs. "Trust me, Thomas. That would never work. Those two would kill each other."

"You're just saying that because you're interested in her," Thomas fires back.

Whoa. This conversation just got all kinds of awkward.

"Thanks for the help, fellas," Bridget yells at us from the road before she stomps in our direction once more.

I suppose I should say something, but I don't know what to say. "You were supposed to wait until Kelsi got here," the Sheriff scolds. "You weren't wearing proper PPE."

Bridget steps closer to all of us as if daring us to take a step back. "I have my nephew's disgusting and sweat-filled jock strap in my Forerunner. Would you rather I strap that nasty contraption to my face?"

The Sheriff looks like someone slapped him. Laughter threatens to burst out of me. "This is the woman you want for your future daughter-in-law," the Sheriff comments to Thomas, who shakes his ducked head vigorously.

Bridget's hand flies to her hip. "Are you suggesting that I'm *remotely interested* in dating Tommy Jr? Because that's *never* gonna happen."

Thomas gives the Sheriff a panicked look before meeting Bridget's eye. "I said no such thing, Bridget. I have no interest in talking about your personal life. But let me assure you that if you keep talking and behaving like a crazy person, no one is going to want to date you."

"Whatever, Thomas. I'm not about to take dating advice from a grumpy old bachelor." Bridget sounds a little insecure. What's that about?

"I'm not a bachelor. I was married!"

"Well, you haven't dated anyone since!"

"I've been busy. Farming is hard work!"

"Not the kind you do!"

Movement behind Bridget catches my eye. Two young women walk towards us: a tall, whip-thin blonde in faded blue jeans which fit her quite nicely, and a shorter, wavy-haired girl with a dimply smile and a few curves. Bridget sneaks a peek in their direction before whipping around to glare at the Sheriff once more. "You called the idiot parade. Why?"

He lays a hand on her forearm as he steps around her. "I'm going to pretend I didn't just hear you say that."

"Go ahead, Sheriff. La la land is a nice place to live," Bridget calls out at his retreating form. She then looks over at me. "Get your tongue back in your mouth, she's married!" I think that barb was aimed at me, but I'm not entirely sure.

I'm already in hot water with this mouthy woman, so I might as well try for boiling point. "Which one?"

"The blonde! So much for having my crop inspection done in a timely manner. I've got better things to do then stand around jabbering about nonsense with the Chamber of Commerce, the Sheriff's department, and the local extension office. Some of us have work to do."

15

"What's the Chamber of Commerce doing here?"

"Scouting out quotes for the local newspaper. Trust me, this dead pig's going to make the rounds. My bad luck is going to spread like wildfire. Do you really think it's glanders?" She looks up at me pleadingly.

I dig my foot in the dirt. I can't believe I want to call myself a liar. "I do. I'm sorry. The only question is, how did it get here?"

Bridget looks off in another direction. She knows something she's not saying. I think the Sheriff knows too.

Just then, the dimply dark-haired girl smiles at me. "Hi, I'm Carli."

"Hello." It's nice to talk to someone who looks happy to see me.

Bridget's halfway between me and her car. Her fists clench at her sides. I feel her tension from here. Is she this upset about a dying pig and a state inspection being delayed, or is it more than that?

"Can you tell me what's going on?" Carli asks.

I'm considering my answer when Bridget strides in our direction. Before I can react, her finger is in my face. I can't help but think of her touching the corners of the cardboard. They were awfully close to the diseased boar. What if the sandwich bag had a hole in it? I tuck my hand inside my suit sleeve and swat her hand away from my face. "Don't touch me with your hands."

She almost looks wounded, but how can that be? She drops her hand to her side and gets all in my face. Her boots bump into the toe of my shoes. Her forehead is at the height of my chin as she stares up at me. "You can't report anything that hasn't been confirmed in a lab." Her warm breath hits me right in the chin.

She turns to Carli. "I mean it. You print anything that isn't the honest truth and I'll be reporting you both for slander." Bridget stomps off in her rubber boots.

# THREE
# BRIDGET

I WALK AWAY from Trevor and Carli as quickly as possible. I can't believe I got so close to that suit. I can't believe he's being so cocky about a diagnosis that hasn't even been confirmed. The odds that the boar has glanders are so miniscule. There are so many other things it could be. I can't think of one of them right now, but that's just because he put that idea in my head. Either way, there's no way in the world I'm giving a single statement to that newshound Carli. If she puts my name on any quotes, she'll be hearing from me directly. I walk over towards Thomas who stands by himself. I'm not about to approach Sheriff Sam, who's talking to Kelsi from the extension office as they hover over my bothersome dead boar.

I step closer to Thomas's right side. "This is so dumb. I can't believe they're getting this excited over one dead pig."

He nods. "Yep."

Great. He's mad at me too. "I'm sorry I yelled at you about Tommy Jr.," I offer.

He swats the air. "It's alright. I know my boy's hard to love." His resignation makes me feel worse. "His mother spoiled him. She made him think he could do no wrong. But

17

she had him when she was 43. He was her miracle child and our only one."

I nod like I understand. I've known plenty of only children and a few momma's boys here and there. They're annoying, sure, but none of them are as awful as Tommy Jr. The only trait I can forgive him for is his IQ level. He can't help his intelligence or lack of it, but what he can help is catching wildlife critters and setting them free in my fields just to get my attention. I move on from that thought, as it makes me uneasy. Part of me wishes Tommy Jr. would meet someone, but the other half wouldn't wish him on any woman.

"I'm sorry I yelled at you about your personal life. You know I shoot my mouth off when I'm angry."

He chuckles. "Yep." He crosses his arms on his big barrel chest and rocks back on his heels. "I've been known to do the same from time to time."

I giggle and look up at Thomas Butros, a man old enough to be my father. His brown eyes, as dark as his wavy hair, give him a boyish look. I don't know what Tommy Jr.'s going to do when his father isn't able to farm anymore. "That's what keeps life interesting."

"It's certainly interesting now," he repeats back to me as we watch Carli talking to Trevor and Kelsi talking to the Sheriff. "Don't write him off as the enemy just because he's an inspector."

I'm embarrassed. "What do you mean?"

He gives me an ornery wink. "You know exactly what I mean. Like I said, I may be an old single bachelor, but I was married once. I know a thing or two about love."

I look over at Trevor standing there in his three-piece suit talking to Carli. There's no mistaking the appreciation written all over his face as he answers her questions. Her flowery dress and cute little sandals are pretty stylish. They remind me that I'm standing here in dirty overalls, a flannel shirt, and rubber boots. I recall the fit I just threw and the noisy threats I issued. I think I'm beyond help in the flirtatious feminine department.

I'll probably have to bulldog myself a man. The thought of chasing Trevor down, lassoing and hog-tying him makes me giggle but then I stop myself. I've completely lost my marbles. What am I thinking? I start walking towards the road where the Sheriff and Kelsi stand a little ways away from the boar. Apparently, she got tired of looking at a dead pig. I don't blame her.

Thoughts run through my mind, and they won't stop. *Why do I listen to Thomas about Trevor? Why would Thomas say that to me? We aren't friends. We're kind of enemies. Did Trevor say something to him about me? Is that what this is about?* "Stop it," I whisper to myself as I walk up the other side of the steep ditch.

"Hey, Kelsi!" I call.

"Bridget," she answers. "What happened with that boar?"

I shrug. "I don't know. Thomas saw it first." Her face becomes more alert.

"That's not what I meant. All I mean is that I drove up and he was standing in my fields. So I went down there and then I saw the boar. It fell over on its side and then it died. It's pretty straight forward."

"Not if it has glanders. That's a major health concern."

I resist the urge to roll my eyes. "I know." I give another glare at the big-mouthed Sheriff. "But no one knows if that's what it is. There's been no testing done for confirmation."

"Which is why we're sending a sample to the lab."

"You already collected the sample? That was fast. I didn't know you kept those collection kits at the extension office."

Kelsi smiles at me. She is so patient that it makes me impatient, which is just stupid. I wish I could stop being so irritable, but everyone's in my business.

"We don't keep the kits in our office. It's not cost-effective. With everything having an expiration date and the need for testing for glanders being almost obsolete, there's no reason for us to keep that sort of testing supply on hand."

"Of course." It makes total sense, and I feel silly for asking. No one says anything. Tension grows along with the silence. "So what is the next step?"

"I'm glad you asked," someone says from behind me. It's nosy Trevor.

I turn to look at him. "I wasn't asking you."

He takes a few steps closer to Kelsi, but it also brings him up right beside me. His arm bumps mine. I feel a jolt of awareness. It's wonderful and terrible all at the same time. I feel like I'm losing my mind. If he felt any electricity, he's certainly not showing it. Fine. I will be as chilled as he is and ignore his touch. I stare straight ahead.

"What do you think, Bridget?" Trevor asks.

*Crap balls.* "About what?"

Carli peeks around him to stare at me like I'm crazy. "Trevor just said his guy is coming down from the state to collect the samples within the hour. Isn't that amazing?"

*No. It's a monumental headache that I don't need.* "Sure. If that's what needs to be done, then I guess it'll get done." *Don't expect me to do jumping jacks or give you applause over a job done that I don't want done.*

"Yeah, that's what I just said," Trevor states. *Darn the man. Why does he have to have the last word?*

"And I agreed," I counter. He smirks at me. Why do his lips have to look so kissable? "Are you about done here, or should I schedule my inspection for another time?"

Trevor starts to lay a hand on my arm but stops. "Hold on a second." He faces Carli. "Was there anything else you need to ask me?"

It's way too easy to imagine smacking him upside the back

of his dirty-blonde haired head. *What is wrong with me?* I start towards my forerunner.

"Bridget, wait up," Sheriff Sam says. I keep walking.

"Bridget!"

I turn to face him with one hand on my car door.

"What's up?"

"I just wanted to apologize for all of this mess." He sounds so sincere that I almost feel bad.

"It's alright. It obviously couldn't be prevented."

"Yes, this is true." He takes a deep breath. "So are you okay with doing your lemonade stand tomorrow?"

"For the fifty-six bicyclists."

"Yes." Sheriff Sam is a handsome man. I've always thought so. His smile takes about ten years off his weathered face. He's about fifteen years my senior, but his no-nonsense thinking and attitude required for his job suggest more like thirty. That can be hard to take.

"I suppose."

"Great." His tone suggests I'm ecstatic to be sitting at a card table all morning providing snacks and lemonade to a bunch of men in spandex interrupting my life with their ridiculous love of racing bicycles.

"Is there anything else?" I open my door.

"Um, no." Sam glances over at Trevor, who is hot-footing it in my direction. "I don't think he's done with you."

Butterflies start at what his statement means to me, but not what he meant to say. This is just stupid. I don't even know the guy. "Yeah. Probably not."

I hop in my car and close the door. Two hands rest on my windowsill. "You got a minute?" Trevor asks. I try to ignore the feeling that I would give him all day.

"Maybe. What's it about?"

He gives me a look. "Your wheat crop."

I fiddle with the inside door handle. "Are you sure you

have time to talk to me? I didn't know if you were done talking with chatty Cathy." I try not to sound as pouty as I feel.

He leans over my window. His form fills my window just right. "Jealous much?"

I frown. I so am. "No. I'm just a very busy person and I have better things to do with my time than wait around for someone blabbing about my business to the local news when it's none of their business because it isn't any business at all."

He dryly pffts. "That's a lot of business." I resist the urge to giggle at his joke. I would find it quite amusing if it wasn't at my expense.

"Whatever. What is it that you need me for?" I regret my words. It's a simple question but something about saying it to him feels intimate.

"I just wanted to revisit the site of the boar. I'm not sure if it touched any of your crop. Your stalks could be contaminated."

His statement, though reasonable and possibly true, flips my switch. "I'm not cutting down any of my wheat crop based on your hypothetical diagnosis! I use every bit of wheat I harvest. It feeds me and this town. I plan very carefully so that none of it goes to waste."

"Would you please get out of your forerunner and accompany me to your fields? I'm just trying to do my job."

I open my door and step out. "Fine. But for the record, I think you're making a mountain out of a molehill."

He stops in his tracks. "I understand the importance of sustainability and provisions, but is the risk of possibly spreading a bacterial disease less important than one harvest?"

My stomach bottoms out at the thought of losing an entire field of wheat. I don't know that I can afford the loss or the reputation of having a bad crop, no matter the circumstance. I hardly want to out Tommy Jr. and his stupidity to the entire town, but at the same time, I'm not taking the blame for this. I catch movement out of the corner of my eye. Carli the creeper is still here. She scribbles away on her little notepad.

I turn and rush in her direction once more. "What are you writing?"

She freezes like a deer in the headlights.

"Nothing." Her eyes look everywhere but at me.

"Whatever you've been writing since my conversation started with Trevor is off the record."

"That's not very specific. Besides he already gave me permission to write what he said," she argues with her little nose turned up.

"Carli, I don't give you permission to write anything I said here today. Zip. Zilch. Nada. Got it?"

Her lower lip quivers. I should care about how harsh I'm being, but I can't bring myself to. She is so flipping nosy.

"Or did I not make myself clear earlier when I told you the first time? Trust me. A one-sided conversation isn't going to make a whole lot of sense. If you write one quote about me in an article, I will out you to the entire town."

Her brown eyes widen. "I have no idea what you're talking about."

I have no idea what I'm talking about either, but I'm going to find the dirt on her. By the look on her face, I'd say there's something big that she doesn't want anyone to know. I don't like resorting to such dirty tricks, but she started it by trying to share my business. It's one dead boar that was barely on the edge of my field, and I didn't even put it there. I'm not having all my hard work and stellar reputation fall apart over one article that carries less than an ounce of truth about a dead pig. I've read enough of her writing to know that's exactly what will happen. "I mean it, Carli. If you write one false word by me or about me, I'll start talking."

"Fine." She rips off pages, wads them up, and throws them at me. "But if that boar turns out to have glanders and it becomes national news, I want that headline!"

I nod. If someone else gets the headline, that's not my problem.

"By the way, I've got dibs on the suit."

I glance in Trevor's direction. By the look on his embarrassed face, I'd say he heard her. I turn back to look her in the eye. "Be my guest!" I could care less if he thinks I'm interested, because I'm not.

The last thing I want him thinking is that I'm fighting with Carli over him. *Dream on, Hollywood.* I glance at him one more time. *You're not that hot.* From the way he tenses up, I'd say he heard my obnoxious comeback. I flash him an ornery grin before turning back to Carli. "It's his decision anyway."

I know I'm twisting the knife, but her gloating is too much to take, just like Trevor in his trooper glasses.

"Hey, Hollywood, you gonna take off those two-hundred dollar Oakleys or what?" I stroll over to where he just dropped to half his height. What the heck is he doing now?

He squats in a catcher's stance in my field. I can't help but notice how well the suit outlines his thighs that look like tree trunks or how well his shoulders fill out the suit coat he's wearing as I walk up on him. He looks so out of place among the stalks. I miss Arnold. He was a lot less distracting.

Trevor, in all his hotness, messes with my concentration. I'm supposed to be mad at him, not attracted. He takes off his sunglasses, unbuttons the top button of his dress shirt, and slides them in place. *Holy moly.* That was the wrong thing to ask him to do. He looks up at me. He's got the bluest eyes I've ever seen. I've never seen the Mediterranean, but I feel like I'm floating. I'm not sure I know what wrecked means, but I think I might be.

His hands rest on the thick strap of his camera resting on his chest. That must have been in his messenger bag that rests against his hip. The sun comes out from behind the cloud and lights up his eyes, making them appear ethereal. I feel all lit up inside and I can't seem to stop it. Embarrassment fills me as I find myself drowning in a sea of blue. He clears his throat. I wake from my daydream.

"I'm sorry, what?" I can't believe I got caught drooling. He gives me a knowing grin. "Stupid sunlight."

"What's that?" I can see that he knows exactly what he's doing.

"I said the sun got in your eyes."

"And how does that affect you?" He knows exactly how it affected me.

"Shut up and put your shades back on."

He doesn't. He just studies me for half a second.

"What do you want?"

"I was asking if you would mind googling on your phone the possible dangers of Burkholderia mallei in crops and if the bacteria can be spread through a plant."

I shrug. "Why do I have to look that up? You're the one who wants the answer and it's your job." I pause. "Although technically it's not your job because you aren't even an epidemiologist." I think of Carli. "You better not have been acting as an epidemiologist when you were all chummy with Carli earlier either, because speaking above the level of your profession and education about things you are not qualified to report on could get you in serious trouble."

He frowns. "I know what I saw." He doesn't sound as sure as he did before.

"Even if you diagnosed it correctly you are not qualified to report it. Just like you're not qualified to report it to the Sheriff's office or the extension office." I hate my level of excitement. "You could be in big trouble already."

He clears his throat. "Issuing a warning in good faith about potential danger that could very well be happening right now as means to prevent further harm from being done is hardly incriminating." He stands up and stares down at me. "Whereas you would rather keep everyone in the dark while feeding me a line of being a philanthropist, but at the same time, you might be poisoning the entire community." His voice is raised.

25

He might be right, but no one backs me into a corner even if he looks dang hot doing it. I poke a finger into his chest. It's rock solid. *Darn it.* "Listen here, *Mr. Bennett.* I will not be bullied into submission. You're the one feeding everyone a line of BS. You're the one spreading fear and throwing big words around when you don't know if any of it is true!" I'm being extremely unprofessional but he's so infuriating. I should stop pointing my finger between his chest and his face, but I can't seem to stop doing that either. "It's so obvious you work for the government!"

He swats at my finger. "Get that finger out of my face! That's the last time I'm telling you."

I drop my hand. I clench and unclench my fists. "Just check out my stalks so we can be done with it!"

He gives me an incredulous look that tells me no one has ever said anything like that to him before. I'm leaving the worst impression. This is a total nightmare. I think of Arnold. He never would have handled this situation so poorly. Trevor and I will never have the rapport that I shared with Arnold. This makes me sad. The silence between us grows. I wish he would say something.

"Would you…" he says. I don't want to know what the rest of it's going to be.

I cough. "Would you like a piece of pie?" I don't know what his next sentence was going to be, but I'm pretty sure it wasn't going to be good for me.

"Excuse me?" Judging by the look on his face, that's the last thing he thought I was going to say.

"A piece of pie. Would you like one?"

A horn honks. We turn towards the sound. Trevor lifts a hand to wave and bumps all along my side. "Who is that?" I ask.

"That's my lab guy. He's here to collect the specimen."

"I guess I'll just be going then. You can call me when you

have time for me." I can't believe how offended and dejected I feel.

"I won't forget about that piece of pie."

I watch him go. There's something about him that keeps my attention. It's more than his confident stride or the way he fills out his suit, but I'm not complaining about the view.

## FOUR
# TREVOR

"HEY, MAC," I say as he pulls up in his F150 King Cab.

"Who's the country girl?"

I watch as Bridget crawls up in her forerunner in her rubber boots and overalls. He's not wrong but his statement rubs me the wrong way.

"She's out working with the crops. What's she supposed to wear, Lululemon?"

He raises his eyebrows. "That'd be a sight to see."

I chuckle at the thought. "Yep."

"So where's this dead boar?"

"Hop out of that truck of yours and come see it."

A few minutes later, he exits his truck in a KN95 mask and latex gloves. He unfolds the disposable yellow gown and sticks his arms in one at a time. We walk over to the dead animal atop the cardboard on side of the road. He looks down at it.

"Do you know the TOD?"

"Time of death."

"Yeah."

"Let me think." I met Bridget at 8:38 AM this morning. I

know this because the second I saw her see me see her, she gave me a dirty look. So about ten minutes after that was when we arrived at the field and about three minutes after that was when I saw the dead boar. "I'd say somewhere around 8:50 to 8:55 a.m."

"Good to know." He gets to work on scraping the blisters around the boar's mouth. I look away. "Do you know how long the boar had been ill?"

I shake my head. "No."

"Do you know how long it had been running around or how much ground it covered?"

"No. But Bridget made it sound like her neighbor's son knows more than he's telling about the boar, so this makes me think that maybe the boar came from their home. If it came from their home, then my guess is it didn't cover much ground before it died in her field."

Mac looks up at me. "If it is glanders and it was intentional, this could be considered an act of agroterrorism."

I nod and rock back on my heels. "I realize that. I don't think that's what it is though." I reconsider the words of her neighbor about his son. "I think this is a harmless prank that went very wrong." Mac looks at me with a strange look on his face.

"I'm saying I think the guy who set the boar loose in her fields was trying to be more of a nuisance than a danger," I continue.

"That's weird," Mac answers.

I tap my toe. "It is, but these are feuding farmers in the middle of Iowa, so..."

"Anything goes," Mac finishes my sentence.

"Exactly."

"You want to help me load this boar in the back of my truck?"

"Not really but I will."

"That's the spirit. But first we gotta hazmat him."

I stare at Mac. "You're kidding."

He coughs from behind his KN95. "I wish I was." He points at my suit. "You might want to lose the suit coat and get your PPE on. It never hurts to be extra careful." He points at his truck. "I've got more PPE in the truck."

I head in the direction of his truck. "So you like this girl," he calls out at my back.

I consider his question. I don't know if I like her, but she has a way of getting me all riled up. She's a contradiction too, though. I can't explain it but there's more to her than just being a country bumpkin. She may wear the overalls and look the part but I would bet she's seen a whole lot more than just Iowa.

She doesn't seem to like my suit, my shades, or my car. I wonder what that's about. And it wasn't my imagination. I think she was jealous of the attention I gave Carli, and the attention Carli was giving me. And she wasn't too happy when she thought I was checking out Kelsi either. All of that must mean something.

Mac and I squat down. We each grab two corners of the cardboard as we lift the dead boar off the ground. Together we carry him over to the truck. "Stop. We have to wrap him," Mac orders. We lower the boar back to the ground.

"Is that proper protocol?"

"I don't know, but I'm not having any part of his disease touching my truck bed."

Half an hour later, we load up the dead boar wrapped in saran wrap held in place with a boatload of duct tape. "Well, that was interesting."

Mac shivers. "Yeah."

I start to remove a glove. "Stop. Don't remove anything until I have a trash bag," he orders.

I wait impatiently while Mac returns with a red biohazard bag. "Put it all in here," he says.

I watch as Mac bags up the PPE. "Hey. Thanks for driving over."

He gives me a grin. "That's no problem. I was at a family event for my wife's family near here anyway, so it was good timing."

I give him a funny look. "You always carry all these supplies around?"

His face turns all serious. "It's important to be prepared. You never know what you'll encounter." He slaps my shoulder. "I gotta run. This has to be taken to the lab within a certain time frame and I don't want my ice in the specimen container to melt. I'll put a rush on the order and let you know as soon as I hear back about the results." He gives me a teasing grin. "Enjoy that piece of pie."

I plan on it. "Yep. See ya later."

I walk over to my Beamer and climb in. I have a crazy urge to pick up a bouquet of flowers. This isn't a date. I want to call the state veterinarian, but I refrain. There's no need to go stirring everything up if my diagnosis is wrong. I know I'm right. I'm 99.5% sure of it. I call my mom to get my mind off the boar.

"Trevor," she answers. There's happiness in her voice. It makes me smile.

"Hey, Mom."

"How is your day?"

I take a deep breath and then another. "I met a girl."

She laughs out loud. "Oh, son. That's wonderful. I've been praying for this day. What's she like?"

"She's a farmgirl."

Mom giggles again. "Is that so?"

"Yeah. She yelled at me." I grin.

"Oh. I think I like her already."

I groan. "You don't even know what happened."

"Then tell me." I proceed to tell her about my morning.

Mom interjects here and there with a little noise or two to let me know she's listening. "And now I'm going to her house for a piece of pie."

"Oh," Mom replies but it sounds more like a question. "That sounds very nice. Is it homemade?"

I don't know why my back is up. "What if it isn't? Are you going to be upset with this girl before you even know her because she can't cook?"

"No, Trevor. I'm not. Calm down."

"Don't tell me to calm down!"

"Trevor Michael Bennett! Don't take that tone with me!"

Fine. "I'm sorry, Mom. I just called to let you know I met someone and now I have, so I think I'm just going to go now."

"Of course. I know you're very busy." Mom's forced cheer is almost too much for me to take. I feel terrible. "I'm so glad you've met someone. She sounds very nice."

*Which part? The part where she yelled at me or the part where she reamed me out for merely informing her she may be poisoning an entire community with her wheat crop?* "Thanks, Mom."

"What's her name?" she asks innocently. I know better. She's going to google her as soon as we get off the phone.

"I'm sorry, Mom. You're cutting out. I've got to go." I hang up. I stare at the dash. I have no idea how much time to give Bridget before I show up at her house to eat pie. This is all so weird. I've never eaten anyone else's pie in the middle of a crop inspection but if there's one thing I know, Bridget isn't just anyone.

I pull into the driveway behind her forerunner and walk up her sidewalk to her front door. Tunes of Patsy Cline float from somewhere in the distance. I ring the doorbell. A dog barks from inside, but it's more of a woof. It sounds like a big one. A foot helps the door open wide. Bridget stands there in her overalls, but her arms are bare. She has flour on her front and a little on her nose if I'm not mistaken. "You're going to have to open the outside door. My hands are covered with dough."

I lift the latch to the screen door and step inside. A big black dog stands in front of me.

"This is Louie," she adds as she looks down at him. "Louie, say hi to Trevor."

I get a bark. I can't tell if it's happy or mad. She leans into me unexpectedly, bumping up against me long enough to kiss my cheek before backing off. Whoa. I feel more from her peck on my cheek than I've felt from lots of kisses I've gotten on the lips. What does this mean?

"See, Louie? He's a friend." The word friend sticks in my ear like an uncomfortable ball of wax. I want to be more than her friend. She turns and walks away like she didn't just break my manly pride in half. Louie flops down on the floor.

"You can shut the big door and come on in the kitchen. I don't want to let the heat out."

I do as she says. I can't help but notice every wall I see is a different shade of green and covered with photos of vegetables. "You're a serious farmer."

She shrugs before she takes a pan off the stove and pours apples into a crust. "Mom always said if you're going to do something, do it right." She looks up at me. "That sounded kind of judgy. I'm sorry. Except that I'm not. I'm my mother's daughter so I cannot apologize for saying that."

I glance around the flowery kitchen. "This room looks different than the others."

She laughs out loud. "That's because it's Parisian. My mother loved all things Paris. My father promised to take her there for their $25^{th}$ anniversary. That day came and went. He did not take her. She was devastated. So ever since that day, my father has bought my mother something from Paris for every holiday, birthday, and Christmas. Any day that is an excuse to buy her something, he does it."

"Wow." I don't know what else to say.

She nods. "I know." She points at the walls and the ceiling. "This is the last room that I have to remodel, but I just can't bring myself to do it. Mom and Dad are in town now. They live in assisted living. If I remodel this room that'll be the last part of them that is still here with me." She rolls out another crust. "It probably doesn't make any sense to keep one room that doesn't match the others, but I don't care."

I think of my dad. "I don't think it's silly. It makes sense to me. We all hold onto those we love in our own way."

She opens the oven and shoves the pie in. "Well, that pie has another forty or fifty minutes to bake so what else do you want to talk about?"

I sit down at her kitchen table. It's disturbing to me how much I feel at home. None of this feels weird and it all should. I've never gotten this personal with any client since starting this job nine months ago. I've never gotten this personal with anyone outside my family, period. "Tell me about your soil."

She blinks. "What about it?" Her voice squeaks. Why should that question make her feel nervous?

"In reviewing your files, I couldn't help but notice your soil grows anything you put your hand to. Every time. The majority of the farmers in this area struggled over the past year or two, mostly due to the drought but you haven't. Why is that? Did you use up all the irrigation water?"

She looks uncomfortable. "Luck of the draw, I guess. And no, I didn't use up all the water. What a thing to say."

I shake my head. "I was kidding about the water. I know you didn't. This isn't the old west where people dam up rivers and creeks to keep it all for themselves. But there's something to your ability to grow crops. I think you've got some secret you're not sharing." I search her face for an answer.

"Maybe I know how to maintain crop sustainability more than the other farmers. Maybe that's it." She leans up against the wall. "Even crops have a certain rhythm you have to follow for the best productivity."

35

I'm not following. She's either full of crap or she's hiding something. "That's an interesting concept. Could you expand on that please?"

She crosses her arms on her chest. "That's not really part of the required material for you to fill out. I don't have to answer that."

Great. I've hit a barricade, but I don't know why. "Obviously that's a sore spot with you. Why don't you want to tell me why your crops do so well? What are you hiding?"

She comes away from the wall and heads for the kitchen sink where her pans sit. She turns on the water. "I'm not hiding anything! I happen to know the questionnaire front and back. I know for a fact what you are asking me is not any of your business."

"Actually, that's not entirely true. There are a few new questions they've reworded and they're open to the interpretation of the inspector, and until I feel you're being entirely truthful with me about the success of your crop yield, I will ask you any damn question I want, and you will answer me."

She whips around to face me. "Fine. But you are not getting any pie. And I will answer your unwarranted questions on the front porch. I'd rather you not sit in my kitchen."

Something flashes outside. We both turn toward the window. "Was that lightning?"

"I believe so."

"But it's midmorning." Thunderclaps. "That was less than three seconds."

"That means a storm is coming."

"That means it's here."

We both step closer to the window. The sky darkens overhead. The electricity goes out. "Oh, dear. It's going to be a long time before that pie is done."

I can't help but laugh. "Yep."

She looks over at me. "I think you should stay."

I can't believe how badly I wanted to hear those words. "Yeah, okay."

"Until the storm passes. It's not safe to be driving in that weather."

"For sure." I don't care what the weather is so long as I'm stuck inside with Bridget Bell.

## FIVE
# BRIDGET

I GLANCE AT THE TIME. It's not even noon. How long will Trevor Bennett be stuck in my house, and how am I supposed to pass the time until the storm is gone? Thoughts of the boar enter my mind.

"I have an idea!"

"What's that?"

"I know a few people at the state. We could call them and ask them questions about the boar." I open my laptop that's linked to my phone about the time I start a three-way Facetime call.

"I don't think that's such a good idea," he says as Karen's face fills my screen.

"Bridget. What's up?" she asks.

"Hey, Karen. I have a few questions," I say before looking over at Trevor who seems to be hiding from my laptop screen. That's weird. "Actually, *we* have a few questions." I motion for him to get in the picture.

"Who's we?" Karen's smile quickly turns into a frown once Trevor's face is in front of the laptop. "Why is Trevor Bennett in your house?"

"It's storming outside," is my automatic response.

"And that explains why he's at your house because..." she prompts.

"He's here for work," I tell her about the time her accusation catches up to me. "How do you know him?"

"We were...we were engaged," she explains.

"Oh." I feel terrible. "I'm so sorry. I didn't know."

"Ewww," Alexia says as her face fills the other half of the laptop screen. "What's *he* doing at your place?"

"He came over to do a crop inspection. There was a dead boar. We fought about it. He came back here for a piece of apology pie from me. Now there's a storm outside," I say frantically. "But I have a question or two. That's why I called. The boar might have glanders."

"It does have glanders," he corrects.

"That has not been confirmed," I argue back.

"Time out," Karen announces. I stop talking. "What is the question?"

I clear my throat. "The question I have is, does it matter if the boar brushed up against some of my crops?"

She shrugs. "I have no idea. That's a question for Trevor. He's the crop inspector. I'm just a veterinarian. I can only answer questions about contagion from one animal to another."

I frown. "Fine."

"Why did you call me?" Alexia demands.

"You are the state epidemiologist," I answer.

"So?"

"So I wanted you to look at the pictures Trevor took," I answer as I make a grab for his phone. "Show them the pictures."

He gives me a look. "Fine, but most of my pictures I took with a camera."

I roll my eyes. "I know you took like twenty-five pictures with your cell phone. I saw you. I swear you got every angle under the sun." I make eye contact with Alexia. "So how do you know Trevor? Did you meet him when he was with Karen?"

She glares at him through the phone. "We dated for a little while," she says. "But then he dropped me out of the blue and stopped returning my calls."

I flush with embarrassment. "I'm sorry." I'm thoroughly annoyed when I realize I've apologized twice on behalf of the arrogant man sitting beside me. He has yet to apologize to either one of my friends.

"Is there anything else you need to know?" Karen asks in a voice that tells me I'll be hearing more later about making her talk to Trevor.

"Um, no." I turn away from him and shoot them both a text at the same time. "I'm so sorry. I had no idea," I type as quickly as possible.

Trevor closes the laptop and leans back in his chair. "Well, that was awkward."

I jump up and start pacing. "It wouldn't be so awkward if you hadn't dated both of my friends."

He stares up at me. "I had no idea they were your friends. I didn't know you when I dated them. We just met each other today."

I shake my head to clear it. "What am I saying? This is stupid. It makes no difference to me who you date."

Hurt flits across his face. I can hardly believe it. "No. I don't suppose it does. Which is why you won't mind if I ask you for Carli's number." I know he's doing it to get under my skin and dang it if it doesn't work.

"I don't have her number, and even if I did, I wouldn't give it to you."

"Why not?" He closes in on me.

"Because...because you seem like the kind of guy who can't commit."

"I was engaged."

"But you broke it off!"

41

"How do you know?"

"Because she just said so!" I'm not about to give up my friend who was seriously broken for a long time after he ended things with her. I want to know why but I'm not about to ask.

"It was the cats."

I have no idea what he's talking about. "Excuse me?"

"Karen. She had too many cats."

I make bug eyes at him. "Didn't you know that when you proposed?"

He shakes his head back and forth. "No. I didn't. When we started dating she had two cats."

"So? What the heck is wrong with *two cats*? Is that really a deal breaker?"

He stares me down until I stop talking. "That's not the end of the story."

I roll my eyes in an exaggerated way. "Not that it makes a difference, but what's the rest of your story?"

"Do you really want to know?" He pouts. I wish I didn't find it so adorable.

"I just asked."

He's quiet for half a second. "Fine, I'll tell you." He sounds like I'm pulling his teeth. "So she had two cats when we met. But then she was up for a promotion at work and she didn't get it."

I give him a glare. "You broke up with her because she wasn't as successful as you wanted her to be. That's a really crappy thing to do."

"No. I just said it was the cats. Can you not hear me?"

"I hear just fine. So she missed the promotion. Then what?"

"She got another cat." As if that explains everything.

"Okay, so now she has three."

He nods. "Yep." He starts circling my dining room table. His finger traces the edge. I can't stop staring at it. "So she had three cats, and then the bachelorette party planning popped up and right after that it was the rehearsal dinner planning and Karen is not much for planning or decision-making. When she gets stressed, she gets another cat. So she got one for the bachelorette party and one for the rehearsal dinner."

"So that's five." I don't think he hears me.

He stops walking and looks over at me. "This is something I didn't know at the time, okay? So I was all set to move in the weekend before we were to be married. I got to her place and she's got five cats in her house and a litter box in almost every room. I felt terrible but I couldn't take it. I had to leave. And so I did." He exhales slowly. "It was terrible timing on my part, and it might make me a bad person, but that's why I broke off the engagement."

I feel conflicted because I understand his point of view even though I wish I didn't. "Did you tell her why?"

"No. I just told her I wasn't ready to be married. I didn't say I wasn't ready to be married to her, and I didn't say one word about the number of cats."

I feel his gaze on me. It heats me through. It feels like he's waiting for me to say something, but I don't know what to say. I feel terrible for her, but I see his point of view. Five cats is a lot if you're not exactly a cat person.

"There have been a few times since that day I thought I regretted making that decision, but now I know I don't."

Half of me wants to ask why and the other half doesn't. I walk into the other room. I don't know what else to say but I need more distance from him. I don't like where I think this conversation is going, or maybe I like it too much. This is all so crazy. We just met.

"Karen is my friend."

"I know. Just like I know I can't be sorry I met you. There's something between us. I know you feel it."

I stand in one room. He stands in the other. We stare at each other in awkward silence for the longest time. He sniffs the air. "I think I smell a pie baking. How is that possible?"

"I have a generator."

"That's very nice." It's as if he's in a trance.

"Yes, yes, it is."

"You lied to me."

My brain searches for an answer to his accusation. He never asked me what my feelings are for him, so I couldn't have lied. Am I that transparent? "About what?"

"About the pie. You told me it would be a long time before it was done."

"An hour is a long time. Do you want me to turn off the oven and ruin my pie?"

"No."

"Okay then."

He walks around the dining room. "Have you always lived here?"

I giggle. "I went to college."

He taps his toe. "Obviously. I meant apart from that have you always lived here?"

"No." I immediately feel a little sad.

"I see." I appreciate his sensitivity to my emotions.

I wipe away the tear that rolls down my cheek. "I lived in a suburb of Boston. I had just opened a specialty shop. It was my dream. It had a tiny office space upstairs. It wasn't meant to be where I lived but I made it work."

"You lived in an office space?"

"I couldn't afford a place to live, and an office space and I wanted to open my business as soon as possible. It was my *dream*. You make sacrifices for your dream." I can't believe how important it is to me that he understands.

"Did it have a shower or a tub?"

I flush with embarrassment. "Not exactly but we farmgirls are resourceful. I bought a washtub for big dogs, and I used that."

He studies me for the longest time. "You're not kidding."

I giggle nervously. "I assure you I am not. You're the only person I've ever admitted that to."

"Thank you for sharing your truth with me." His tone of voice tells me he's not really that thankful.

I shrug like it's no big deal, but it is. Every time I took a bath in that tub, I was so ashamed I didn't have a real tub. I told myself that it was a small price to pay for being able to keep my business open. For the most part, I don't regret it. Opening that business made me realize if I worked and believed hard enough, I could achieve whatever I set my mind to.

"What was your shop?"

Half of me is tempted to tell him something really strange. "It was mostly for advertisement. I was a graphic arts person. I designed book covers."

"I'm sorry to ask but why did you need a store to advertise? Isn't that something you can advertise on the internet?"

"You can, but the suburb I lived in was like one of the five places in the U.S. that's like a book lover's mecca. It was sort of like the word nerd capitol. Everything book-related is there. So it was a big deal to be able to open up a storefront to advertise my art."

He gets an ornery grin on his face. "Did you do like romance novel covers?"

"Not like you're imagining." The way he asks makes me feel embarrassed.

He raises his hands in protest. "Okay, okay. Just asking. There's no need to get so defensive."

"I'm not defensive. I'm just saying what I did takes creativity. It's not as easy as you think to try to encapsulate a novel with one picture. Sometimes the author knows exactly what they want, but sometimes they have no idea. And sometimes there's creative differences. That's when it gets challenging."

"How much personal freedom do you get in creating a book cover?"

"As much as the author allows. I also like reading the blurb that goes on the back. That's also part of what I do."

He studies me once more. It's hard not to fidget beneath his steady gaze. "You design book covers, you grow any crop you want, and you drag diseased pigs out of fields," he says in a low, sexy voice as he steps closer and closer. "Is there anything you can't do?"

My feet feel like they're glued to the floor. "Dance," I say without thinking.

He chuckles. "Excuse me." He stands in front of me.

I look up at him. "I have no rhythm. I'm not joking."

His hand falls on my waist. His other one remains in the air. "Take my hand." I do. "Dancing is just you following my lead. Let's go."

I put my hand in his with a giggle. "There's no music."

He tugs on me until I run smack into him. My cheek brushes his chest. It's wonderful. "We don't need music to move." We move slowly around the room. His feet shuffle. I struggle to mimic his actions. "You're a terrible dancer."

I lay my head on his chest. "I know. I did warn you. But I can learn."

## SIX
# TREVOR

I DON'T THINK I've met anyone who dances as awkwardly as Bridget Bell. A few years ago, that would have been a deal breaker, but I'm older now. There's nothing that could pry my hands off her perfect waist. Her toes bump against mine more than a few times, but I don't care.

"So why did you stop dating Alexia?"

"I don't know. It wasn't one particular thing. She just wasn't right for me."

"That's not entirely fair."

"Probably not, but at least I stopped seeing her before we got serious. Besides, it's not like she didn't know I started dating her too soon after I broke off the engagement from Karen. I wasn't ready. I tried to tell her that, but she's pretty persistent when she wants something." I try not to blush.

"Yeah, I guess." I can't believe she didn't take my head off for saying that about her friend.

"How'd you meet them?" I ask her. "Do you know them through ZOOM calls or work?"

She leans back far enough to steal a look at me. "I went to a conference put on by the KAHLD organization. Karen and Alexia were there. They were like the only other women there at the unofficial "under thirty" table. It didn't take long for the three of us to hit it off over the open bar, which was the highlight of the night. I think that was probably the first and last KAHLD meeting that allowed alcohol to be served."

It's hard to imagine Bridget enjoying their company. She seems so different from the two of them, in a good way.

"Alcohol and tipsiness. The secret to forming friendships."

She steps on my toes on purpose. "Don't go there, mister, unless you want stats on how many men bond over a six-pack of Bud Light on a daily basis. Trust me, I know. If there's one thing the men in this community are experts at, it's buying beer and sitting around and drinking in their spare time." I believe her. Those two things were my father's middle name.

She nods. "So, yeah. That's how we met. Before the night was over, we exchanged contact information and we've been friends ever since."

"Lucky me."

She smacks me on the chest. "Not everything is about you. You act like the three of us got together and decided to date you one at a time. It's not like that."

"Are you saying you want to date me?" I tease but I'm not joking.

She digs her chin into my chest. "Trevor. Shut up and dance with me."

"Yes, ma'am." I can't help but notice how well she fits in my arms. By the way she snuggles into me as we shuffle around her dining room, I'd say she feels the same way. My mind strays back to her story of owning her own business. Even though it's disturbing to think of her taking a bath in a tub on the floor, I can't help but admire her determination. "How did you cook without a kitchen?"

"I slept on a cot. I had an ironing board that unfolded from the wall. I kept a toaster oven in my bedroom. My diet was pretty repetitive, boring, and budget-friendly. I kept a coffee pot downstairs on the small counter. There was one room downstairs and one room upstairs. The bathroom was also downstairs."

"Wow. You weren't kidding. That is minimal living. So you're saying you had to take a bath in the tub downstairs; like in your office area." I try to picture where she hid her tub during office hours.

"I wasn't about to run a hundred plus cups of hot water up the stairs."

"One-hundred cups," I say, followed by a whistle. "Dang, girl. That's a lot of pouring."

She giggles. "You're telling me. It took just as long to fill that tub with water as it did to bathe in it, but at least I had hot water. You probably think I'm crazy." She lays her cheek on my chest.

"Driven people get things done. I don't think you're crazy. I think you're determined."

"Thank you. You're being more than generous."

"Ha. Imagine if more people in this world were as brave and motivated as you are." She tenses beneath my touch. "I'm not that brave."

I can't explain it other than to say it feels like she's hiding something again. But what?

"I have my secrets." I wait for her to elaborate but she doesn't. I'm not sure what to do.

I glance down at her. She's looking up at me. I move slowly towards her because I'm pretty sure that's what she wants. I really want to kiss her but what if it's too soon? And what about professionalism? What am I doing? Why am I over-thinking this? It's just a kiss that's about to happen between me and a woman who could very well be the one for me.

*Hold up. The one.* That must be why my stomach feels like there's a knot that's being tied tighter and tighter. I think I might throw up. I stop moving forward. I focus on dancing and the thoughts whirling around inside my head, making me feel insane.

*Come on, Trevor. Man up. You've got a beautiful woman in your arms waiting for you to kiss her. So just go ahead and do it already. Where's your confidence?*

I could do it. All I'd have to is to move a few more inches. Doubt creeps in all over again. But what if things go wrong between us and she gets me fired? She wouldn't do that because she's part of what's happening right now. It takes two to tango. Her breath smells so sweet and it feels more wonderful than anything I've ever felt on my face. I'm hovering like a crazy person. The art of anticipation will be lost if I don't do something. *Do anything besides standing here like a statue.*

A knock at the door makes us both jump. She flies out of my arms. A look of hurt crosses her face. Great. I messed up the first real moment we were about to have. I'm such a coward. I know who I want, so why didn't I go for it? She opens the door. A guy soaked to the skin stands there with a black cowboy hat in his hand. He lifts his head and gives her a knowing grin. *Dang it. Who's this guy?*

"Randy," she says. "What are you doing here?" Her tone is too neutral. I can't read it.

He steps inside and shakes his wet head like a dog. "I just stopped by to check on you. I know how much you hate storms."

"Thanks, but I've got company."

Randy looks past her to me. His eyes were all warm and concerning turn as hard as granite in about half a second. He strides across the room with his hand extended. "Hey, I'm Randy." He grips my hand like he's trying to smash it to smithereens. I will myself not to wince.

"Good to meet you," I lie between my teeth. "I'm Trevor."

He releases my hand and takes a step backwards. "Are you here for business or pleasure?"

Wow. That was unexpected. I search Bridget's face for an answer. She ducks her head for half a second before clearing her throat. "As you can see, I'm just fine. Thanks for your concern, Randy, but you should be going now."

"If you say so," he says. It's clear he has no intention of leaving. He leans down as if to kiss her. She turns her head. His searching lips land on her cheek. Her smile appears forced as she gives him a small shove towards the door.

"Go on home, now. I'll be fine. Really."

His gaze stays on hers. "If you need anything I'm just down the road."

"I know," Her words sound a little less kind and a bit impatient. "You take care now. You'd better get home before the storm gets any worse."

"Yeah." He starts unbuttoning his shirt. *What the heck is going on here*? He has it all the way off in about two seconds. This man has no shame.

"What are you doing?" she asks as he holds out his shirt to her.

"I was wondering if you could dry it for me before I go home is all. Wearing a wet shirt could give me pneumonia."

She snatches the shirt from his hand. "Randy, you live right down the road, and you have your own drier!"

If he hears the scorn in her tone, he ignores it as he plops down on her couch and sprawls out. Great. Tarzan plans on sticking around and ogling Bridget, and he's not even trying to hide it.

"Do I smell apple pie baking? You know that's my favorite!"

I do my best to stare him down with my dirtiest look that I reserve for desperate hound-dogs who shamelessly use every tool they can think of to get a woman, but he completely ignores me.

"I bet you're using your family recipe. You know, the one that everybody wants. This storm reminds me of the night we met, you remember that." Something white hits him in the face.

Bridget is back. She stands at the end of the couch. "There. Now you have a shirt to wear home!"

He tugs it over his head. It's a little tight and a whole lot of short. I resist the urge to laugh.

"What is this?" he whines. "I can't wear this. What about my shirt I just gave you?"

She stands over him. I can't see her face, but I can tell by the way she stands she's not happy. "Randy," she enunciates as if he's a naughty schoolboy who doesn't speak English and who's about to be sent to the corner. "You gave me your shirt. You asked me to dry it. When it's ready to be picked up I'll text you and you can take it off my clothesline. You cannot have any of my pie. I didn't make it for you."

He stands up, grabs his cowboy hat off the coffee table and jams it on his head. "So much for being neighborly. I just wanted to be sure you were okay."

She stares up at him with her hand on her hip. "I appreciate your concern. I am fine, which I already told you. This is the second time I'm asking you to leave, so please leave."

He gives me one last glance and backs up as slowly as a sloth. "If you're sure."

"I'm sure," she agrees.

His exit is beyond awkward, but he finally gets to the inside door and opens it. The wind howls outside. "You'd better get going before it gets worse." She sounds like a broken record, but it doesn't matter because I don't think he's listening.

I'm not sure how she'll react, but this guy doesn't seem to be getting the picture. I walk up behind her and wrap an arm around her waist. She lays a hand on my arm and leans back against me. I rest my chin on the top of her head. "It was nice to meet you, Randy," I say.

His hand slams against her front screen door, sending it flying. It whaps against the outside of her house before slowly coming back. He stands on the other side, glaring. "So that's how it is!"

"I'm sorry, Randy. But I've moved on," she says. He spins on his boot heel. My eyes widen as I read the front of the shirt he put on backwards. "Build a bridge and get over it" fills my eyes. I try to hold in the laughter that wants to spill out of me. Bridget closes her inside door on the jacked-up truck that peels out of her driveway in the middle of a small hailstorm. She flips the lock before turning to face me.

Her face is flushed with embarrassment or something else - I don't know, but it's too much for me to handle. I missed my chance while we were dancing but I'm not missing another one. The force of the storm outside may be part of the madness running through me but I'm going with it. All I know is I have to know the feel of her lips. I dive in.

Her breath mixes with mine and it is absolute perfection. I never knew a kiss could feel like this. I feel every part of her kiss from my head down to my toes. Bridget Bell is the most fascinating woman I've ever met. I don't know what I want exactly, only that I want more.

There's pressure on my chest about the time she bumps her head on the door. My hands fly off her waist and out of her hair. Her hazel eyes are wide open. She laughs. I didn't know what I expected but it wasn't that. I think I feel wounded. "That's a first."

Her fingers cover her mouth. Her ornery smile peeks out at me. "I'm sorry. It was just so unexpected, the force of your..." she stops and clears her throat. "I mean everything came at me all at once that's all. You're...you're very solid."

I think it's a compliment but I'm not sure. "Okay." I suppose there are worse things I could be called. "So I'm guessing he's an ex-boyfriend." I'm not sure I want to talk about him. Especially now.

Her hazel eyes cut to the side. She makes a whooshing sound with her mouth. "Yep. That's Randy." She cocks her

53

head a little. "I'd been in town for about a year. I guess I got a little lonely. He was always at the bar-and-grill whenever I went there for take-out. We just started talking here and there and he kind of wore me down."

"He seems nice enough."

She nods. "He was alright until he got comfortable."

Comfortable could mean so many things. "Translation please."

She rolls her eyes and rocks back on her heels. "Comfortable as in he started expecting me to fix every meal he ate, do his laundry, call him in the morning to wake him up, sit with him 'til midnight every night down at the fishin' hole, and watch him drink a six-pack."

I cough. "That's a bit much."

She taps her fingertips on her elbows. "Well, I thought so. So after two-and-a-half weeks of feeling like his mother, I called it quits."

"And how'd that go?"

"About as well as telling a three-year-old he can't have his favorite John Deere tractor toy."

I laugh out loud. "You're pretty funny."

She lets out a long sigh. "It wasn't funny at the time. I swear between Randy and Tommy Jr. I practically lived in my field. One of them was always doing something to mess with my property. I finally had to call the Sheriff." A buzzer goes off in the kitchen. "Oh, hey. There's my pie." She jogs back to the kitchen.

"Why don't you like to call the Sheriff?"

"Because I'm mostly a country girl and I'd rather take care of my business myself." I walk toward the sound of her voice. She shuts the oven door with her foot and plops a pie down on a hot pad on the island.

"You're a one-woman balancing act." I watch her set the pie down while she extends one foot in the other direction.

"Don't make me laugh or I'll drop my pie." She opens the fridge and pulls out item after item.

"What you doin' now?"

"Making home-made whipped cream to go with the pie. That's the right way to eat it." She tosses her hand on her hip. "You're getting the whole Bridget Bell dining experience."

I think she's flirting with me. I know I like it.

She measures and dumps before turning on her Kitchen-Aid. "The other reason I don't like calling the Sheriff is because I feel like sometimes he thinks I'm trying to think of reasons to call him and that's just not true."

Relief floods me at her last statement. I didn't think she was interested in Sam, but it's nice to hear. Randy's words come back to me as the smell of a delicious-looking pie surrounds me. "So you have a secret family recipe?"

"What?" She sounds so alarmed. "Who told you that?"

I point at the pie. "Randy said something about your pie when he was here."

She visibly relaxes. "Oh, yeah." She waves her hand in the air. "That's just a recipe passed down from generation to generation. I couldn't even tell you where it started. Randy tends to exaggerate when it comes to my baking skills. I think it's because he'd do just about anything to get me to cook for him."

I nod. "Well, I can understand that." I snatch a cookbook from a shelf and flip through the pages. "I can cook recipes that are simple because I know how to read, but that doesn't mean I like to."

"But you can cook?"

"Yeah. I can cook."

Bridget rushes me, lays a hand on each side of my face and gives me what I would call a smooch. "Thank you!" She steps back over to her Kitchen-Aid. "It's almost done," she says as if she didn't just *knock my socks off,* in the words of my grandfather.

"What was that for?"

"For cooking, and for possibly stepping outside your comfort zone."

I can't help but grin. "If I teach you how to run a chainsaw, can I have another one of those?"

She tosses her head back with laughter. "Um, no. I'll leave the heavy lifting and big blades to you, and I'm not ashamed to say so."

"Fair enough."

## SEVEN
# BRIDGET

I NEVER THOUGHT I'd have a stranger in my home for this long, or that it would feel like I've known him forever when in fact we met just this morning. It feels so strange. I can't believe Randy practically threw himself at me in front of Trevor, or that Trevor backed me up against the door with that steamy kiss.

My face flushes at the thought of him coming at me like that. All alpha male. That was so hot. I glance in his direction as he flips through the cookbook. He doesn't act like a take-charge macho guy, but those demanding lips of his turned me inside out. *Mercy*.

"Looks like my whipped cream is done," I announce a little too loudly. His answer is an ornery grin. I think he has an idea of how nervous he makes me. The turkey.

"So what's your secret?"

"For what?"

"For the success of your crops. I don't think I've ever seen anyone who has the variety of crops that you do in a confined space at such a high frequency and production rate."

I try not to let my emotions show on my face. This is a common question that I've heard from more than a few people, and it's been happening more and more. I have a secret fertilizer that I've concocted and perfected since I moved back home but I'm not about to tell him that. I don't know why everyone needs to know, and it could just be a coincidence. It hasn't had enough time to be tested. I just have to be patient. I don't know if I want to sell a product if it's not the real deal.

"My mother always told me if you work at something for the benefit of others it will almost always work out." I try not to sound preachy. "That's why I grow all those crops. They're not just for me and they're not just for profit. A certain percentage of whatever I grow goes to the local food pantry for their fresh produce section. The rest of it is sold to local people. I have a list of regular customers. They appreciate being able to buy local and not having to drive an extra 35 miles just to get their food supply. They know I don't use any pesticides or chemicals that would harm whoever buys my produce."

"But how do you do it so well?"

"Maybe I'm just really good at what I do because I like it so much, and maybe I'm just a really hard worker."

"Thomas Butros doesn't have the luck you have. His fields are right across the road from yours. So what's the difference?"

"I meditate." *I totally don't.*

"What's that look like?"

His question is honest, but the look on his face insinuates he doesn't believe me.

"Just how it sounds. I go out into the fields every day twice or three times a day depending on the health of my crop and the season. In the morning, I do rise-and-shine yoga to show the crops how to grow tall and strong. I open my arms to the sky and show them how to produce the fruitful bounty that feeds us all." I can't believe how much crap I'm making up.

"During the evening, I show them how to sway with the

gentle breeze as it blows over through the stalks." I demonstrate even though I feel like an idiot.

"Yeah, sure. If that's how you want to play it."

I sniff. "I'm not playing. Modeling growth for your crop is totally trending right now. It's the latest craze in the ag world." I'm about to lose it. I can already feel a fit of giggles coming on.

"If you don't want to tell me your secrets about growing a great crop, fine, don't tell me. But don't lie about it."

I feel a little bad when he accuses me of lying, but the giggles are here, and I can't hold them in. I whip around to turn the other direction while I try to gather myself by leaning over the counter and stomping my foot on the floor like a wild woman. "Fine."

I try to hold in my laughter. "No, I don't do crop yoga. That would be ridiculous." The giggles pour out of me. I turn sideways and straighten up. I will myself to be done with the giggles. It mostly works. I raise a finger and give him a glance in the corner of my eye.

"But you can't tell me that people don't do that sort of thing because I'm sure they do."

He chuckles and cocks his head back. "Too true. You could make a TikTok or two. It could be like a whole new thing. People would probably watch it."

"Don't tempt me." I dish him up a piece of pie and scoop some whipped cream on top before sending it his way. "There you are. One piece of apple pie as promised."

He takes a big bite and groans. I can't believe how good it feels to know he likes my baking. "Oh, wow. This is soo good. I don't think I've ever had pie this good, and I've had a lot of pie."

I can't help but giggle at his strange statement. "Is that so?"

His blue eyes fix on mine. I kind of forget what we were talking about. "It is so. I happen to be a huge fan of small-town cafés and apple pie. I always get the same kind of pie.

*Always*." He's so emphatic. "I like to compare." He points at my pie. "This is hands down the best apple pie I have ever tasted and that's a fact."

My heart sings. "Thank you. I'm glad you like it."

He takes a smaller bite. "I do. I truly do."

"So how did you become a crop assessor?"

He hunkers over his plate of pie like I'm going to take it back. "It's kind of a funny story. I grew up on a farm. It wasn't my favorite thing to do. I can't tell you how many times my parents fought because my mother wanted to travel but my dad was always tied to the house because of all of our animals. So it was always a point of contention between them. She would get so upset and it could last for days or even weeks. So it was never fun watching them fight or dealing with the emotions that followed. And for me, it was all about baseball. I loved playing ball, and I was pretty good at it. There was a traveling team in our town, but Dad wouldn't let me try out because it meant we'd be gone every weekend. So I played on the town rec team instead."

He laughs but I can tell he doesn't think it's very funny. "One year I even tried out for the traveling team, and I made it. I was sixteen years old. I was so excited. I thought if I tried out and made it Dad would have to let me play because I was old enough to go on my own. I could drive." He clears his throat. "But he didn't. He told me I had family obligations to the farm." He leans back in his chair. "After that I never played baseball again. I resigned myself to working on the farm for my parents until I went to college. After that I decided I would never live on a farm or be tied down to anything like that ever again."

Silence follows. I feel like I should say something, but I don't know what to say. He knocks on the tabletop. "But that's not what you asked. You asked how I became a crop assessor. When I went to college, I was interested in becoming a teacher." He shoots me a charming grin. "Believe it or not I like kids. I like the idea of working with them." He takes a deep breath. "But teaching requires more creativity than I possess, and after taking a few classes I began to understand that. And then I met a girl who I fell pretty hard for. I thought she was the one and she thought so too, but that was before she fell in love with our lab teacher."

"Whoa. That's quite the story. I'm sorry about all that."

He grins. "Yeah, well that's not the end of it. Our lab teacher was a *woman*, so that was a hard kick in the crotch for me."

He taps his fork on his plate. "So actually, I've been engaged twice. I kind of know how it feels to have your heart broken."

*I guess so.* "I'm sorry. I don't know what to say."

He shrugs. "Life can be like that. The unexpected happens and it knocks you on your ass." He raises his fork in the air. "But the one good thing about life challenges is it makes you realize what's important and that you can live through something you never thought you could. You find out you're stronger than you thought and that things aren't as big a deal as you thought they were." He takes a deep breath. "Don't get me wrong; it's a big deal when an engagement ends unexpectedly but it's not the end of the world. There are worse things than getting dumped for someone else."

"At least she dumped you for another woman. I mean that should tell you there's nothing you could do about that."

He chuckles. "I guess that's true." He takes another bite of pie. "At the time I just felt stupid because I couldn't believe I didn't know. I was twenty-one years old and feeling pretty cocky. I thought I had my whole life planned out. I thought I knew what I wanted and how it was going to go." He takes another bite and looks down at his plate. "It turns out I didn't know much."

"Well, who knows what they want to be when they are twenty-one? I thought I was going to be like a book cover designer for some famous author one day, or that I would design a killer logo that would be so attention-grabbing that everyone would want to buy the product. I never thought I'd end up in my hometown growing wheat and produce to feed like half the community and then some," I say. "But I am. And I love it. And I can't imagine doing anything else. There's something comforting about knowing your neighbors. It gives you peace of mind."

He takes another bite. "I suppose. But doesn't it feel weird to know that the majority of this town has watched you grow up? Like they've seen you have your first crush. They know if you've broken the law or dated someone else's boyfriend."

I cough. "I guess my life's not all that interesting. I can't say I've done either of those things."

He gives me a grin. "Well, that's a good thing. I'm just saying that like if two women in this town fought over the same man and one of them ended up with him and the other didn't, *everyone* would know about it because it is such a small town. Or like if someone was wild in their younger days but then they settled down, or if they found God and changed their ways, everyone would know their past life unless they moved away."

I nod. "This is true, but would that be the worst thing? I mean you gotta hope that most people are just like everyone else. They know people make mistakes, but they also know that our mistakes don't define us as a person. It's whether or not you *learn* from your mistakes that counts. Sure, some people are fortunate enough to go through life and not make any major mistakes, but some people aren't. I think that's part of being human. None of us are perfect."

"Well, I can't argue with that, but this pie of yours is darn near perfect. Is there any chance I can get another piece?"

I glance outside. I can't believe I didn't notice the storm is all but gone. "The weather's settled down. I think it's safe for you to go wherever you need to go next." I wrap up the rest of the pie. I just remembered I've got somewhere I need to go, and I need to get there before Trevor does. I want some answers from Tommy Jr. about that boar.

He stands up from the bar stool he was sitting on. "I'm sorry. I guess I lost track of time. I'll just get out of your hair and be on my way." His voice is as stiff as his posture. I didn't mean to give him the brush-off, but I'm not sure I want to start anything with him either. He's my crop inspector.

"Sounds good." I try to forget he kissed the crap out of me or that I really liked it. "I'm sure I'll hear from you soon on that pig."

"Yep." He grabs his John Deere hat and fits it to his head. "See you around." He sounds dismissive and not at all like someone who shoved me up against my front door less than two hours ago. I wish he weren't so sexy. I wouldn't mind him staying a little longer, but I've got things to do.

I wait anxiously for him to disappear from my driveway. As soon as I see him head down the road, I grab my pie and run out to my forerunner. I take off in the opposite direction. I park a little ways down the road from Thomas's back door. I feel a little crazy as I creep up the side of his house and knock on his front door.

The door opens. Tommy Jr. stands in front of me. "Hey," I say.

"What are you doing here?"

I hold up my pie. "I brought some pie."

He looks all dejected. "My dad's not here right now."

"Well, this pie is for you *and* your dad." I open the screen door and scooch by him. "I'm just going to put it in the kitchen." I try to act braver than I feel. Tommy Jr. seems harmless enough, but I've never been alone with him in his own home.

"That's nice of you. Momma used to make me pie. I miss her."

The sadness in his voice makes me want to cry. "I

63

remember her pie. I miss your mom too. She was a real nice lady."

I clear my throat and force myself to look up at Tommy Jr. He's a giant. "Earlier today a wild boar died in my fields. Do you know anything about that?"

He shakes his head back and forth. "I sure don't."

"Are you sure?"

His fist pounds on the countertop. "I just told you I don't, so I don't." His face turns red. "Why's everyone always accusin' me of things? It's not fair."

I take a step back and glance past him at the front door. He's blocking the doorframe. I look over at the back door. "Well, I hope you enjoy your pie. I'm just going to go now."

"You could stay and have some with me."

"That's very nice of you, but I gotta go."

Tommy reaches for my wrist. I dodge him at the last minute. "I've really got to be going, Tommy. Someone's coming to my house soon. They're expecting me." I feel bad lying but he's making me nervous.

"You can't go if you can't leave." He's got a cringey smile.

My stomach ties itself in knots. I think I'm going to be sick. "Tommy!" someone yells.

"Yeah, pop?"

"Leave Bridget alone. You're scarin' her."

Tommy's bottom lip juts out. "I was just tryin' to be nice. She wouldn't let me." He stomps out of the kitchen. I breathe a little easier.

"Hey, Thomas," I respond.

"Bridget. What brings you over?" Suddenly the room looks a lot smaller.

"I need you to talk to you some more about this dead boar. I need to know Tommy's involvement in it."

"Why? So you can report him as an agroterrorist? It was an honest mistake."

I roll my eyes. "Relax, Thomas. I don't think he's an

agroterrorist, okay? You have to be really, really smart to know what you're doing in that respect. Tommy doesn't have a clue. I bet he ordered that boar from somewhere in Asia to possibly mess with me, but once he saw that it was sick he had to set it loose in my fields where it fell over and died."

My simplistic explanation makes sense, but it's not the end. "The problem is, that's not the end of his mistake. It's just the beginning. This thing is going to blow up in both our faces if I'm not careful and I don't know how much I can do to stop it, especially if it's got glanders."

He starts pacing. His hands seem to have a mind of their own as they move around. "If I could stop my son from ordering things off the internet I would. I've already blocked the Wi-Fi from our home. I can't very well tell the town librarian to not let him on the internet. It wouldn't be fair for me to ask Jane to cancel the Wi-Fi for everyone because my son can't control his impulses. He's just doing these things to get your attention. You know that, right?"

I can't believe he said it out loud. I had my suspicions but still. I didn't want to know. Because now I can't unknow. "I didn't ask for your son to be interested in me."

"I know that!" he barks in my face. "I didn't ask for my son to be someone who doesn't listen once he gets an idea in his head but that's who he appears to be."

My head aches from trying to find a solution to Tommy Jr. and his crazy behavior. "Well, it better stop soon. Otherwise, he might end up in jail."

"Why would he end up in jail?"

"They might fine him. And if he doesn't pay..." I'm grasping at straws.

"That could be a problem. I don't have a bunch of cash lying around. What about you?"

*What the heck*? "What about me?"

"Do you have any cash lying around?"

"No, but even if I did, I wouldn't give it to Tommy."

65

"It's your fault he acts so crazy."

"No, it isn't. I've never done anything to lead your son on."

"You brought him some pie!"

"I was just being *neighborly*! Can't a girl be a good neighbor?" I demand, but I feel bad. I brought the pie over to mend fences, sort of. Mostly I wanted to get information about the stupid boar because I'm 99.5% certain Tommy Jr. did it. I don't know what proving he did is going to fix, but I just need to know.

A knocking at the door interrupts our glaring contest. "There's someone at your door," I say.

"What?"

"There's someone at your door." I grab him by the arm, startling us both. "If it's Trevor don't tell him I was here."

I'm heading to his back door, but my curiosity gets the better of me. I do something I'm sure I'll regret. I slip inside the closet and sit down on a bucket. The sharp edges cut into the back of my legs, but I don't dare move. I listen as hard as I can. All I hear is mumbling.

"Why isn't the kitchen closer to the front door?" I whisper. My breath catches when I hear Thomas's familiar heavy step followed by a scuffling of Trevor's slick leather shoes as they walk back in the kitchen.

"Trevor, what a surprise," Thomas says in a more pleasant and enthusiastic voice than I have ever heard. "What can I do ya for?"

"Thanks for asking, Mr. Butros. Can I call you Tom?"

"Sure. That'd be just fine."

"Great. Well, I've been thinking long and hard about how that boar with glanders ended up in Bridget's field. Do you have any ideas?"

"I'd love to help you, but I have no idea," I hear Tom say. "I heard a few counties over they had some strange algae in some of the lakes and ponds. Maybe this boar got into that and brought it over here. You know they run faster than most people would expect. Those suckers can cover a lot of ground in a short amount of time."

"But don't they usually run in packs?" Trevor asks. I stifle a giggle. I can only imagine the irritation Tom's trying to hide right about now.

"That's true, that's true," he stutters. *Calm down, Tom. Being nervous just makes you look guilty.* He clears his throat. "But animals are just like people. Once in a while you get a lone wolf. Maybe he went out on his own and got separated from the rest of 'em. Heck, I don't know." I think I see a shrug through the slats. I look down at the floor. If I can see out, they might be able to see in.

"That's a pretty good explanation, Tom, and I'm tempted to believe it, but I just can't quite swallow your carefully concocted load of crap."

*Whoa.* Why is Trevor being so aggressive? That's not going to help anything and it sure won't get Tom to open up to him.

"Are you calling me a liar?" Yep, Tom's getting plenty angry.

A chair moves across the floor. "I'm not calling you anything, but that oversized crate with a big red EXOTIC ANIMAL stamp on the side of it probably is. I don't think it's mere coincidence that huge crate in your yard looks about the right size to house a boar."

"That crate could have held anything. You don't know how long it's been there."

"Oh, but I do, and I have documentation of it. I took a few photos as proof. There's a date on it and everything." My mind races. What the heck? How did I miss a huge crate laying around in their yard? It must be on the other side of the house.

"That's just the date you took the photo. That doesn't prove anything."

Trevor rolls his eyes. "You need to quit overlooking Tommy's bad behavior or just plain looking the other way. If you looked closely at the box, you would see there's a shipping date stamped on it in bold back letters. Heck, it's practically branded on there. It's nothing I could make up." His tone sounds more resigned than confrontational. At least he's on his way to calming down. "It's obvious Tommy imported that boar from somewhere in Asia."

Ha. I totally called it. I hear tapping. I think it's his foot.

"Now why would he do that?" Trevor asks.

I hear someone rustling about and then there's a thump. I reach for the doorknob. What if Tom is having a heart attack? "As long as I've known my son I've loved him dearly, but I don't understand him," I hear Tom say. I drop my hand back to my side. "He gets foolish notions in his head, and he just acts on them. I've tried to slow him down. When I couldn't get him to stop ordering ridiculous things online, I shut down the internet access to my house. It slowed him down until he discovered the public library. I can't very well ask the local librarian to disconnect her internet access because of my son's bad habits."

There's only silence. I can't believe Tom is telling Trevor all his business.

"Anyway," Tom continues. "I think the boar just got away from him. I don't think he meant for it to get into Bridget's fields."

"I know for a fact your son has been harassing Bridget for some time now," Trevor argues. "I hear she's had an unusual amount of pests." Oh crap, why did I tell Trevor that information about Tommy and why is he telling Tom? There's no need to hash all that out now. That won't help anything. I need to stop this crazy conversation. But how? I can't just walk out of the closet. That would be too weird.

"You've seen Bridget's extensive gardens. All that crop is bound to attract the local wildlife," Tom argues.

"While it's true she can grow just about anything and her crops are quite productive, I find it hard to believe her fields can bring in raccoons, opossums, moles, and armadillos all in the same week," Trevor argues. "You're just being stubborn and unreasonable."

There's more silence. I can't believe Trevor is being so insulting to Tom while sitting in his kitchen. "Well, you can't say my son isn't persistent," Tom tells him.

"Most of his pranks were harmless, but this one crossed a line. Glanders is a very serious situation. We can only hope this boar didn't spread it to other animals before it died."

"Now look here. My son would never intend to infect half the livestock in the county with his carelessness. What's really going on is he's feuding with the girl he's had a crush on since the second grade. I realize my Tommy has gone a little too far with his desire to get her attention, but can you blame him? She's the whole package. She can bake. She's not too hard to look at and she's a terrific farmer."

*Oh, my.* I'm sure Tom is just trying to be nice, but I did not need to hear any of that coming out of his seventy-four-year-old mouth. I wish I was sitting anywhere but in Tom's closet on a bucket trying to ignore the canned goods cutting into my back. If I move, they might all fall. I'm undeniably stuck.

"You make some good points," Trevor agrees. What the heck does that mean? Is he being serious or just accommodating an old farmer? Is that really how Trevor sees me? "But she can be awful contrary and bull-headed." *Screw you, Trevor.* "And she has a terrible temper and a short fuse." My jaw drops. I reach for the doorknob again. I can't believe he's being so harsh. I'll show him what kind of temper I've got. "Between the Forerunner she drives and her overalls, I'm not so sure she's looking to date any guy." *Yes, I am, Trevor Bennett, and I think you know that since we shared such a hot kiss not that long ago.* My head is so hot. It's about to explode.

"Mmm hmmm," Tom answers to Trevor's last statement. I can tell from the sound of Tom's voice he doesn't believe a word of what Trevor just said about me not wanting to date guys. "Well, aside from advising other farms of general precautions to take and signs and symptoms to watch for, what do you suggest I do to ensure the appropriate measures are taken for the safety of the livestock?"

Trevor coughs. "So you do understand the severity of the situation." There is irritation in his voice.

Someone laughs. I think it's Tom. "Listen here, boy. Just because I talk slow and use small words don't mean I'm stupid. I just don't see any point in speaking faster than you can understand."

Oh, no. Now Tom is throwing shade. "Speak as fast as you want, Tom, I can keep up," Trevor fires back.

"I'm sure you can, and it's a good thing because I'm not done with asking questions." There's a pause. "What are you going to do with Bridget's field? She feeds the majority of the town with her crop yields." *Finally. A question I want the answer to.*

"Does she run a stand at the farmer's market then?" *I already told you that, Trevor. Were you not listening to me?*

"Yep. She sells everything at cost. She's not out to make a profit." *Well, gee, Tom. That's very generous of you to say.*

"You think she should charge more?"

"I do." My jaw drops. What? *That's not what he tells me.* "That woman is sitting on more secrets than is healthy for anybody." Oh, crap balls. Why did Tom have to bring that up?

"Like what?" Trevor asks. I really think I should come out of the closet now, but I can't. I passed the point of embarrassing to downright sociopathic and jeepers creepers two subjects ago.

"All kinds," Tom answers in a raised voice. "Bridget Bell makes the best darn salsa and jams I've ever tasted, and don't get me started on her *pies*. But she won't share the recipes with no one. Folks say she has some little room in her basement with no windows. They say she does all her cooking and canning down there at two in the morning so no one can catch her at it. She probably has her recipes locked up in some sort of safe."

"And then there's her crops. She's never had a bad year, even when everyone else does. I swear the woman could grow anything she put her hand to." He pauses. "Some people say she's got some kind of magic fertilizer, but no one knows what it's made of."

I blush so hard as I sit here listening to this strange conversation about me, I think I might be having a hot flash. The trouble with Tom's accusations is there's too much truth in all of them. There's a reason I hold all my cards so close to my vest.

It's the same reason I'm so enraged and disappointed with Tom for selling a big percentage of his water rights to the Saudis and letting the government put windmills on some land he inherited out in western Kansas so he can collect a fat check every year while pretending that he doesn't do either, because then he couldn't blame the government for his problems.

*Commercialization and greed.* Those two words may as well have been swear words in my house growing up. My dad was the son of a blue-collar worker who worked for everything he ever had, and he passed the value of a hard day's work to his son, my father, who passed it onto me. "Don't be a sell-out, Bridget," my father said to me when my parents moved to town. "I'd rather you sell the farm than commercialize our family secrets."

My lips trembled and my chin shook, but I promised Dad I would honor his request. And I prayed I would always have the courage to trust in his words of assurance that the Lord would provide as long as I lived a true and honest life. I close my eyes for half a second and resist the urge to change my position on the hard bucket, as my leg has fallen asleep clean down to my foot, but I don't dare move. *So much for being honest.* I keep quiet so I can continue my eavesdropping.

The noticeable silence cuts into my memories. The longer it goes on the more I'm confused. *What is going on out there? Where did they go?* I want to get up, but I don't dare. The last thing I want is for Trevor to discover me hiding in Tom's closet. The minutes drag by. They feel twice as long every time I sneak peeks at my wristwatch on the underside of my wrist. About the fourth time I check it, I vow not to look at it again. *This is madness.* I'm on second 333 while counting in my head when the door is flung open. The look of shock on Tommy Jr.'s face is priceless. It almost makes up for every time I've chased some wild critter of his out of my field.

He looks like he's about to pee himself. I stand up from the stool in an indignant fashion before marching past him as if this is my house and he's the intruder. "It's about time," I say to his gaping fish mouth as I walk by. I stare out the front windows of the house and note Trevor's state vehicle is nowhere to be seen. I slip out the living room window just to be safe and take off across the yard for the nearest tree line. I dart through the woods and double back to my waiting vehicle parked out of sight.

"Dang that boy. Trevor Bennett is going to be hard to shake, but I've always enjoyed a challenge. Now that old Tom spilled all my secrets to Trevor, I've got to dispel all those crazy notions I'm sure are flying around in that handsome head of his. I may as well invite him to dinner. There's no harm in baking up a meal that will knock his decorative socks off," I say to no one but the person who grins back at me in my rearview mirror. "Oh, Bridget. Get a grip."

The guy has me hiding in pantries and climbing out of windows. It's safe to say I'm in way over my head with Trevor Bennett, and I don't mind it one bit.

# EIGHT
# TREVOR

MY HEAD IS SWIMMING after that crazy conversation with Tom. If I didn't know better, I'd say someone was nearby. Someone who smells like apple pie and flowers, but that's crazy. There's no way she would be hiding in the old farmer's house. That's beyond creepy. Then again, it's no creepier than having some secret room in her basement to cook things in at two in the morning like a witch with a cauldron. I shiver in my heated Beamer seat.

"Stop thinking such crazy thoughts. That old farmer is just telling tall tales. That's what people do when they live in the middle of Iowa wheatfields. They make up strange stories about their neighbors because they're bored out of their skulls. This place is so crazy it has me talking to myself."

My phone vibrates on the seat beside me, interrupting my one-sided conversation. I hit the talk button. "Why didn't you tell me how hot Trevor is?" *Whoa. What is going on?* Someone just called me hot. I think that's Bridget's voice. Why is she saying this to me?

"If I had known he could kiss like that..." she stops talking. I open my mouth to tell her she has the wrong number, but then close it. If I answer, she's going to hang up the phone. I need to know what she's going to say next. Who does she think she's talking to? "Ugh, I sooo didn't need to know it."

I'm staring at my phone so long I almost miss my turn. Wait a minute. Is that her Forerunner flying down the road? I turn in that direction. What the flip is going on here?

"And now I have to work beside him on this project and pretend I don't want to jump him. I'm sorry to call you about this. I don't mean to be insensitive. It's just I can't call Alexia because she's still hung up on him, I think. And she's mad at me for liking him on any level." She stops talking again. I glance at the phone and then back at the road. She's sitting in front of me at a STOP sign. This is too weird. Why isn't she moving? Her words are stuck in my brain.

"You can go now." I smirk.

"I'm go-ing!" She punches the gas and peels out.

Gravel sprays the front of my Beamer, and I can't even be mad about it. The accidental confession she just made runs circles in my brain. I must be on cloud nine. I swear my ego could fill this entire car. There's no way she did that on purpose.

I stare at the phone. I think I hear breathing, which means she hasn't hung up. "You gonna hang up now or do you have more to say?" I feel incredibly insensitive. Loud music blasts at me. I can't help but smile. This goes on for a few minutes. It's crazy but I won't be the first one to hang up. Loud music doesn't bother me. Nothing bothers me. Bridget Bell is crazy about me, and she just admitted it.

"So we've got some stuff to figure out and talk about," she blurts through the phone. "So you want to come over for dinner tonight or what?"

"Since you asked so nicely, sure. Why not?"

"It's a home-cooked meal. Take it or leave it."

"I'll take it, but this isn't the way to your house."

"I'm going to the grocery store. I have a few things to buy. If that's okay with you."

74

"Sounds good. I've got a few things to buy as well."

"Oh, *goodie*," she says in a voice devoid of emotion before hanging up on me. Ten minutes later, I follow her into a parking lot. She's out of her car. It looks as if she's jogging into the store. I get out and walk briskly across the lot like a normal person who isn't chasing after someone who just called me hot. On accident. But it still counts.

I stride across the store, feeling like a maniac as I scan the aisles. I discover her in aisle seven. I mosey after her.

"Hey, darlin'," I tease. "There you are."

She bumps me with the end of her shopping cart. "I'm not your darlin'."

I throw my hands in the air. "Ease up there, tiger. I was just kiddin' around." I raise my eyebrows at her while she glares at me. "You're the one who called me hot. That could lead a guy to think a few things."

She waves her hands around in circles. Kind of. "You know what? Just erase that whole conversation from your brain, okay? It wasn't meant for you to hear. I thought I was calling Karen, and I will not feel bad about it or answer for it to you. Now, let's decide what we're making for supper. I'm not having you think I'm some sort of crazy kitchen witch. You can help me make a casserole and see for yourself my kitchen is just like anyone else's and so are my baking habits."

I stare her down. "Why would you call yourself a kitchen witch, and what makes you think I think anything of the sort?"

"Because I heard…" I've never seen someone look more guilty than she does right now.

"You were there." I knew I smelled her. I'm not completely crazy.

She hides behind the boxes of pasta she takes off the shelf. Her face is blank when she turns to look at me. She shakes a box of pasta on each side of her face. "Whole wheat or white?"

"You heard me."

"I heard no such thing. Do you want whole wheat pasta or white? I need to know."

I point at the white pasta box. She drops the whole wheat in the cart. "I need to know if you were hiding in Tom's closet today." I'm pretty sure I already know the answer.

"I plead the fifth." She attempts to walk around me with her shopping cart. I lay two hands on it.

"I'm not moving."

"Fine. Don't move. You can eat a peanut butter and jelly sandwich for all I care. I was going to make my grandmother's super-secret casserole. It has a little magic in it, they say. But now you'll never know." Her warm breath hits the side of my neck. *Holy guacamole.* I'd follow this woman into any basement, kitchen witch or not.

"I like casserole." I grab the back of the cart and trail after her. "What else do we need to get?"

"Nothing. I don't feel like shopping or baking anymore." *Boy this girl is moody.*

"Okay fine. Well, I'll just get my own ingredients for the casserole I make and I'll meet you at the house!" I call. She's already at the end of the aisle. And then she's out of sight.

I head back to the boxes of pasta on the shelf to look for the elbow macaroni. "Aha."

I reach for it and clutch it to my chest, debating whether or not I need a basket. I only need two more ingredients. I turn to go forward and she's right there in front of me. "What the heck are you doing creeping up on me like that?"

Her hazel eyes are wide open. She looks nervous. She steps close to me and lays a hand on my arm. "Could you please kiss me?"

"Excuse me?" Just then I see Randy, the ding-dong cowboy, heading right for us with some woman clinging on him.

"Are you making him jealous?" I realize I don't care as I toss the box of pasta into her shopping cart. If she wants me to kiss her in the middle of aisle seven at the grocery store, then I

76

guess I will. I snake an arm around her waist and jerk her flush up against me. My other hand flies to the back of her neck. My lips head for that perfect jaw line I've been wanting to taste ever since we kissed the first time.

I bury my nose in her neck for half a second while I inhale her sweet flowery scent that is unique to just her. I swear I could find this girl in the dark. I know the second her dainty fingers dig into my shoulders. *Holy Toledo. We're made for each other.* I feel it in my bones. My lips finally meet hers. If I didn't know better, I'd say the tile floor just shifted beneath my feet. Our kiss goes on forever, but at the same time it's not nearly long enough when she backs away just a little. Her hands slide down my chest.

I turn to look for Randy and his girl, but they're long gone.

"Thank you," Bridget says, all prim and proper.

I reach up and take her hand in mine. "You're welcome." I look her in the eye. "Now. Are we doing your casserole or mine?"

I think I see appreciation in her eyes. I am so awesome. "What are you making?"

I set a foot on the cart. "I have a special casserole I call Tuna a la broke college student. It has four ingredients. Tuna, elbow macaroni, peas, and cheese. You just stir it all together, pour it in an 8x8 and bake it."

She wrinkles her turned-up nose. "That sounds kind of gross."

I shrug. "It's an acquired taste. It gets better with every dollar you save."

She giggles. "Fair enough." She squeezes my hand. "Lucky for you, I'm not a broke college student and I have some experience in the kitchen." I didn't think I could like her more than I already do.

"Do you now? I like experienced women. I hear they're great teachers."

She lets go of my hand and slugs me in the shoulder. "That was kind of cringey."

I take her hand in mine once more. I swing her hand up and kiss her knuckles. "I'm sorry. Let me rephrase. What kind of oven do you have?"

"I have the latest model. It's electric and it even has a timer," she purrs.

This is the most ridiculous and fun conversation I've ever had with a woman. "Ooh, e-lec-tric. I can't wait to get my hands on it." We walk down almost every aisle in the store before we get to the self-checkout. "If you bag, I'll pay."

She gives me a look. "Are you sure?"

"Definitely." I catch Randy in the corner of my eye. "This is our date night. I insist." I then give her a quick peck.

She lays a hand on my cheek and gazes at me adoringly. This girl can really put on a show. I just wish it was real. "Thanks, hon," she says before scanning and bagging our items. We walk outside. I keep a hand at the small of her back all the way to her Forerunner. We put the groceries in the back seat. I turn to walk away when she grabs me by the collar and draws me in. The back door is still open. She leans up against the side of her Forerunner. I don't see anyone but I'm not fighting it.

Our kiss starts out hard and fast, but it's as if time slows down when I feel her hand cup the back of my neck. Her lips soften beneath mine. She lays a hand on my forearm while she stands on tiptoe to get closer than I thought possible. What is happening? I can't believe I met her just this morning. I used to laugh at anyone who talked about love at first sight but now I'm not so sure. All I know is I'm nowhere near ready to walk away from this girl.

I grip the side of the seat behind her shoulder. I can't believe I'm the one who's backing away. "Bridget," I growl.

"Hmm," she says. I want to dive back in.

"What are we doing?" What am *I* doing? I don't care what

78

this is. I don't want it to stop. Why did I just ask her the question girls usually ask me?

She traces shapes on my chest through my shirt. "Just having a little fun. Is that alright with you?" I can't believe how much it hurts to hear her say that.

"Is that all this is?"

She tilts her head to the side. "I've known you all of a day, Trevor. What do you think this is?"

I back away. "I don't know." I lay a hand on my chest where hers just was. "I'll see you at the house." I slink down into my Beamer and shut the door.

"This is all her fault. If she hadn't called me and said all that stuff, I wouldn't even be thinking of her in that way." I rehash what she just said compared to what she said when she called. "She did only talk about how much she likes kissing me, so I guess that doesn't really mean she wants any sort of commitment, but she doesn't strike me as the kind of girl who only wants to have fun either, so what was that all about just now," I mumble to no one. "This girl has me talking to myself more than I ever have before. This is insane."

I hit the steering wheel as I drive down the road. "Who meets the girl of their dreams over a dying boar? That's the most unromantic thing I've ever heard."

My head is still racing when I pull into her driveway. "I guess I just act like everything is cool when I go in there." I get out and walk up to sit on her front porch.

"Where is she?" Half an hour passes. She's still not here. "Did she get lost on the way home? She doesn't seem the type to chicken out," I grumble right about the time she pulls up the driveway. I walk over to help unload her Forerunner.

"Let me give you a hand."

"Thanks, but I've got it." She sounds like a robot. What the heck happened between "hot lips hottie" in the grocery store and "chill as a cucumber" at home?

79

"Okay." I take a few steps back. "Just let me know when I can come in."

"What's that supposed to mean? I invited you to cook with me and that's what we're going to do, unless you don't want to."

"I'm up for the task if you are."

"Fine."

She opens the door. A big black dog shuffles by. "Come on, Louie. Come on outside. Go be a good boy." she croons.

I rub his head a few times. "Hey, King Louie."

"Don't patronize my dog!" she barks.

I can't help but laugh. "I wasn't. You're awful touchy. Did something happen on the ride home?"

"No," she spits out. "Why do you ask that?"

"You're about 40 degrees colder than you were in the store parking lot."

"That was all for show." With her back to me, she sets things out on the counter. "You knew that."

"Was all of that for Randy? Were you making sure he knows you're over him, or was it to make him jealous?" I'm not sure I want the answer.

Her hazel eyes widen. "Of course, I'm not trying to make him jealous. Oh, crap. Why didn't I think of that? Do you think he thought I was trying to make him jealous?" There's no disguising the worry in her tone.

"I doubt it. I mean, he was gone by the time we came up for air."

She blushes. "I'm sorry I attacked you. It's just that girl he was with. She's so awful. I don't want her thinking I'm pining for her man, or whatever."

"Pining," I tease. "What kind of word is that?"

"Longing. Wanting. Waiting. Pining. They all kind of mean the same thing, so whatever."

"So you don't like this girl being with him."

"No. That's not what I said. I just said she's awful and I

80

don't like her. I could care less who he's with, except that he knows I don't like her which is why he's with her, and she knows I don't like her which is why she's with him. Do you get it?"

I try to sort through her rambled answer. "Basically, you're saying the only reason they are together is centered around you and your intense dislike of this girl."

"Bingo."

"May I ask why you don't like her?"

She nods. "She's a two-timing boyfriend and would-be husband stealer. Every woman in this town doesn't like her and she knows it, but she doesn't care. She doesn't want someone unless they belong to someone else."

"Well. If that's true that's too bad." I close in on her. "I'll be sure to keep my eye out for her." We stand so close our shoulders touch.

"Why's that?" She goes still. Her voice is so quiet.

"She thinks we're together. I'd hate to disappoint you by falling for her hidden charms."

She shrugs. "It makes no difference to me who you date. It won't be long, and you'll be on the road again and I'll still be here."

Her tone sounds like she doesn't care but I think there's more there than she's letting on. "I've had girlfriends before, you know."

"I know. Two of them are my friends."

"That's not really fair to throw that in my face. I dated them before I knew you. We've already had this conversation."

She slams the pasta box down on the counter. "You're right. Let's just not talk about any of that. Let's just cook. There's a big pot in that cupboard. Get it out and fill it three-fourths full of water, please."

I crouch down and open the cupboard. There's a ton of pots and pans. "Which one?"

She lays an elbow on my shoulder and leans over me. I

wish I could plug my nose. She smells so good. Her hand flies out. "That one. Right there."

It's so tempting to grab the smallest on the shelf just to irritate her, but I don't. I drag the big pan off the shelf and take it to the sink. I proceed to fill it with water. By the time I get back to the stove there's another smaller pan on the back burner. It's full of red sauce. "Where'd that sauce come from?"

She gives me a wink. "That's my secret sauce. And no, I'm not telling you what's in it. It's a family secret." She points at the stove top. "Turn that up to high. Drop a pinch of salt in your water and then pour the pasta in. Once it gets to boiling we're going to boil it for another five to seven minutes like the box says. In the meantime, I need you to chop the chicken breast up so we can cook it in the skillet with some mixed veggies."

"And then we just mix it all in with the sauce and the pasta and bake it?"

She nods. "Pretty much."

"That sounds easy enough." I unbutton the bottom of my sleeves so I can roll them up. I'm not getting chicken juice on my dress shirt. I grab a cutting board that hangs on her wall and the knife stuck to the magnetized bar near it. Minutes later, I'm back at her side. "Where's your cooking oil?" I say near her ear.

She jumps. "Personal space." She points to a cupboard across the room. "The oil is in there."

I pour a little in the deep skillet before picking it up and rolling the oil around. I turn on the heat before scraping the chicken off the cutting board in. The look of surprise on her face is very satisfying. "You thought I was bluffing about cooking, didn't you."

She makes a face with her lips. "May-be. I've had guys tell me before they can cook and they couldn't, so..."

I stir the chicken chunks around in the pan with a spatula.

"Well, I'm not most guys." I try to sound as unoffended as possible.

"I'm beginning to see that."

I wave the spatula in her direction. "Just like you're not most girls. So tell me about this secret fertilizer of yours. What's that all about?"

She freezes up right in front of me. "Why are you asking about fertilizer?"

I turn away from her and continue moving the chicken around. "Where are the veggies? I think it's time to add them."

She reaches over and grabs a package off the counter before ripping it open and all but dropping it in the pan. I step back. "Hey, watch it. You're going to get oil on my dress shirt."

"Then take it off."

"Fine. I will." Grease pops out of the pan and splatters my shirt. "Dang it." Some of the grease gets on my forearm and it's hot.

Her hand is already on the dial that she turns down to simmer before she's back to me. Her fingers are nimble as she unbuttons me. "What are you doing?" My voice is all husky, but I can't seem to change it.

"Fixing your shirt." She practically shoves it off me. "Go stick your forearm under cold water. It's red."

I stand here in my ribbed cotton tank top staring at her. "Thank you." I will my feet to move, but I'm taken in by her hazel-eyed stare.

"You're welcome." She walks clean around me on her way out of the kitchen with my shirt in hand. I can't help but notice how quickly guys start stripping in her presence.

## NINE
# BRIDGET

"HE'S JUST A MAN," I mumble as I stand in the laundry room sprinkling the grease spot with my special powder mixture that's good for removing stains. I scrub at it with the damp scrub brush.

"What am I doing? Is there really such a thing as love at first sight? Great-great-grandpa always said there was. Maybe it runs in the family," I mumble to myself as I shrug out of my overalls. I stand here in my cotton tee shirt and underwear. I grab a pair of cotton shorts off the drying rack and slip them on before heading back to the hot kitchen that got a lot hotter once Trevor stepped in it. I smile to myself. I can't help it. He's so stinking cute. And he knows his way around a kitchen.

"Where's my shirt?" He looks like he's pretending to not notice I'm wearing shorts. I'm dancing inside.

"I put some cleaner on it so I'm letting it soak." I pretend that I don't notice how good his forearms look.

"Is that another family recipe you're not sharing?"

I tense up while trying not to. "Maybe."

He levels me with a look. "You do realize your family keeps more secrets than most."

"Maybe. But at least they aren't bad ones."

85

"Exactly," he says triumphantly. I don't understand his enthusiasm. "Why not share them with other people if they could benefit them?"

I spoon up a noodle and take a bite of it. "Soft enough." I try to pick up the pan of boiling hot noodles.

"Could I please do that?"

"You do realize I live at home, and I do this by myself when you're not here." I step away from the pan.

"I do, but I'm here now. So let me help." He lifts the pan like it's nothing. "Where am I taking this?" Steam hits him in the face. He holds the pan farther away from himself.

I snag the colander hanging above the island and race to the sink with it. I hold it by the end of the long handle. "Pour them in here, please."

"Teamwork." He gives me a wink. Once the pan is empty, I move the colander out of the way of the deep sink.

"You can just set that pan in the sink." I set the colander full of noodles on the drainer side. I hurry back to the stove to dump the sauce in with the chicken and veggies. "We need three or four cups of noodles to pour in this pan."

"How do you know if it's three or four?"

"I eyeball it." I turn the oven on 375.

"The index card said to bake it at 350."

"Yeah, I know but these garlic knots cook at 400, so I'm improvising."

"Don't you mean compromising?"

"It's however you see it."

"Fine." He dumps four cups of noodles into the skillet.

"You were supposed to do them one cup at a time!"

"Improvise!"

I stir the mixture in the pan. "We may not have enough sauce. It might come out kind of dry."

"Guess we'll find out."

"You're so annoying."

"Happy to oblige."

He's as mouthy as I am. I might be in trouble.

I look over at him. "You never finished your story about why you became a crop assessor."

He looks all sorts of irritated. I think he knows I'm avoiding his questions. "It's not that interesting. Basically, when I was in that lab class, the one I already mentioned where my fiancée fell in love with the lady lab teacher; well, she couldn't help but notice I have a strange knack for identifying plants and recognizing plant ailments. She was the one who suggested I go into the field of study that I'm in. She seemed like a smart enough person so I took her advice."

"The woman who stole your fiancée is the one who directed you into the career that you are in."

"Yes."

"Well, that is sort of fascinating. I can't believe you listened to her. Was this before or after you realized she broke up your engagement?"

"It was after actually. My fiancée told me she was in love with someone else and that I was on the wrong career path. Then she told me she thought I would be miserable if I went into teaching."

"And you listened to her? I mean, you listened to them?"

He dips a finger in the sauce. "I did. I was feeling very vulnerable about a lot of things. It was a night of revelations you might say." He takes a deep breath. "Even though they both hurt me I still respected them as observative, analytical people. I felt my ex-fiancée was the one who knew me best even if I didn't know her like I thought I did, and I felt like my professor wouldn't lie to me about my abilities in horticulture."

"Well, you're a better person than I would be. I think I would've given your fiancée the boot and told them both they could keep their stupid opinions to themselves."

He laughs at me. "I suppose that would've been a good answer too, but at the time I was really struggling, and she seemed so sure of herself. I guess I just wanted someone to tell me what to do with my life." His blue eyes search mine. Whoa. Is he doing that right now? Is he asking me what I think he should do about us? He can't be. There is no us. We haven't even been on a proper date. But I have talked to him about more things that mean something than any other guy ever in my life. This is all so confusing.

"And it was nice to hear someone tell me I was good at something," he confesses. "After going through all that, I really needed some validation."

"Are you always this open?"

His jaw tightens. I think I just asked the wrong question. "No. I usually never am. You just seemed like a good listener. I'm sorry if I read you wrong." Sorry seems to be the last emotion he's feeling.

"You didn't." The oven timer goes off. I've never been so happy to open an oven door. I need a break. Things are getting too intense.

Minutes later, we sit across from each other at my little round table in the kitchen. "I'd like to say grace."

He closes his eyes and bows his head. I do the same. "Dear Lord, thank you for the food we are about to eat and thank you for this time we have together to get to know each other better. Thank you for the rain we received today. Thank you for watching over all the animals. Thank you for your love and kindness. May we show others the love you show us. Amen."

I break my garlic knot into a bunch of pieces before forking one and dragging it through my casserole sauce. I glance up to see Trevor doing the same thing. I can't help but laugh. "Great minds think alike." I hold up a piece of sauce-covered bread on the end of my fork.

He bumps my bread piece with his. "To good taste." His blue eyes light up. I try not to stare as I wait for his reaction to my secret sauce. I am not disappointed when he leans back in his chair and lays a hand on his stomach. "Good gravy, you could bottle that up and sell it. I'd pay for it all day long." He ducks his head over his plate to take another bite.

I do the same. The table is quiet for a few minutes while we really dig into our plates. Several bites later, he gets an ornery look on his face. "Well, I'd tell you what I discussed with Tom at his home today, but I don't think I need to." He studies me. "What made you hide in his pantry?"

I try not to wither beneath his searching blue-eyed gaze. "If I was hiding it's only because I'm the curious sort. Maybe I just wanted to know what you were after." I fork another bite of casserole. "How much trouble would Tommy Jr. be in if agroterrorism was suspected?"

"That's actually very hard to prove, especially when a bacterial infection is tied to an animal."

I can't believe how relieved I feel. "Tommy Jr. is a royal pain in my butt, but I don't think he has any intentions to do me harm." I give Trevor the eye. "I can't believe you told old Tom what I said about his son and the wildlife. I told you that in confidence."

He fidgets in his chair. "I didn't mean to do it. It just slipped out. He made me angry because he was trying to deny everything." He shakes his head. "He's part of the reason his son does everything he does. No one holds Tommy Jr. accountable for his actions."

"You sound like a parent."

He pales a little. "That's not funny."

I snort. "It's a little funny." I drag my bread through the last bit of sauce on my plate. "You're the one who said people should be held accountable for their actions." I make a little dig which probably isn't fair, but I don't really like how his face paled at me joking about him being a parent. "Are you a dad or something?"

He tenses up in his chair. "No." He looks a little sheepish. "Why would you ask me that?"

"You reacted a little weird to my comment about being a parent. I wanted to know why."

"You're very intuitive. Are you sure you're not a cop?"

I stick out my tongue. "You're the inspector, not me." I fire back. "I'm just a simple Iowa farmgirl."

"Ha. You're anything but simple." He fiddles with his fork. "That's the problem."

I blush at the compliment. "Thanks."

# TEN
# TREVOR

WE STAND at the sink together washing dishes. I look over at her. "You weren't too impressed with me when we met this morning, were you?" I watch her face.

She wrinkles her nose. "Between your citified clothes, over-priced shades, and shiny shoes, no. Not to mention that hot little car of yours. It might look good on the highway or a paved road, but it's not exactly made to drive down dirt roads."

"You've given this some thought." I try not to feel so hurt.

She shrugs. "I'm just answering the question. I'm just saying - why would you buy a Beamer if you knew you'd be driving out in rural communities?"

I look back at her. "Not that I owe you any explanation, but I was supposed to have a desk job. I'd just gotten the job. I live with my mom because..."

Her jaw drops. "You live with your mother?"

"I'm paying off college debt. And it's a separate apartment attached to her house, so it's not like it sounds."

"Fine. *Maybe* you're not a momma's boy. I haven't decided yet."

"You're awfully judgy." I'm only half-joking.

"I know. It would be my hamartia if I were a hero, so it's lucky that I'm not."

"Sounds good to me." I have no idea what she's saying. "What would my hernia be?"

She busts out laughing. "You mean hamartia, the fatal flaw that takes you down."

"Aha. That's easy. I hate washing dishes. I would rather scrub a toilet bowl. The dishwater is just so grimy and full of everyone's saliva." I give her a friendly nudge. "But your presence makes it a little less than detestable so thanks for that."

She blushes. It's adorable. "Thanks. But technically hating washing dishes can't really be a hamartia because that's not like a personality trait or whatever."

I exhale slowly before digging out my smirkiest smirk. "Fine. Then tell me, what is my hamartia, since you're Queen Smarty-pants."

Her hazel eyes look me over for less than half a second. She looks a little unsure until her eyes stop on my belt. They light up. She's on full alert. I brace myself for an incoming missile. "I don't know you well enough to answer that question but given that you are so fixated on exposing my secrets, I'm tempted to say it's greed."

That's the last thing I thought she'd say.

*What the heck?* "What makes you think I'm greedy?"

"You're a walking status symbol with that fancy car of yours and your Oakley sunglasses." She grabs my belt and turns me around while turning it inside out. "Ha, just what I thought. You're wearing a Gucci belt. Nothing screams status louder than that." She sounds so sure of herself. I hate to burst her bubble, but I'll give it my best shot.

"How do you know I didn't find it at Goodwill? Or what if someone gave it to me as a gift?"

She blinks and chews on her inner cheek for half a second. "Huh-uh. Nope. I reject your counterpoint. If you bought it at a thrift shop, that means you were still after the name, and if

92

someone gave it to you that probably means they know you well enough to know what the name means to you." She narrows her hazel eyes at me that resemble a shade of jade. "Someone could have spent their entire paycheck on that gift for you. You should have given it back."

This girl is unbelievable and stubborn as a mule. "You're making a lot of assumptions over one item of clothing," I fire back at her. "And maybe someone gave it to me because they were trying to impress me because *they* like brand names." My voice grows a little louder. "And maybe I'm the one who had to google the brand name to know how significant it's supposed to be." I undo the belt and whip it off before dropping it on the floor. "There. Take it. I don't want it anymore." I'm well aware I'm being more than a little irrational.

Her hazel eyes widen in disbelief. "What in the world am I supposed to do with a man's Gucci belt?" Her face is flushed. She's so hot.

"Hang it in your trophy case of other items you've shamed people out of. You're the most infuriating woman I have ever met."

Her tiny hands are clenched in fists at her side. Every muscle from her jaw down to her ankles is tense. "Ditto." She takes a big drink of water and sets down her cup. I pick it up and drink the other half. She stares at me in confusion. "I thought you had a thing about other people's saliva."

I raise one eyebrow at her. "Everybody makes exceptions, Bridget. You're my exception." I can't believe I'm falling for someone who is so exhausting. No one says anything for a second or two. Our latest discussion rolls around in my brain as I stare at the Gucci belt lying on the floor. The side of my brain that won me the title of Championship Debater in high school that is forever tattooed on a plaque that hangs proudly in Mr. Boller's office just woke up. *Oh, snap.* I'm not done. Not by a long shot.

"Maybe I just came from an Ag convention, and they were handing out Gucci belts as souvenirs."

She makes a half-snorting sound. "Yeah, right. Like Gucci would ever want to set a gold-plated toenail inside an agricultural convention. Get real."

Bridget doesn't know it yet, but her half-hearted challenging statement has just been accepted. "You don't know that. Gucci wheel covers for John Deere tractors might be the next thing that trends on Twitter and the gram." I have no idea what I'm saying right now but it sounds good to me.

She bursts out in giggles. Dang. Seeing her crack up in the kitchen and holding her stomach was so worth my ridiculous sputter. I can't help but grin all the more. "I'm just sayin'."

It takes a few seconds, but she manages to get a hold of herself. "Fine, you win this round. If I allow you to put that stupid designer belt back on, will you shut up about it?"

"Maybe." I lean over and pick it up off the floor. "I live with my mother." I turn away from her to put myself back together. "You can't call me a total snob if I still live at home."

"Yeah, that is a bit contradictory." She leans against the counter with a sigh. "That puts a dent in your Beamer-driving, Gucci-wearing, agricultural gigolo image." There's a definite bite to her tone that cannot be ignored.

"Whoa. That was a real zinger." It kind of came out of left field. I thought we were halfway getting along. "I thought you said you were working on being less judgy."

She ducks her head and stares at the floor while I stare her down. "Yeah, I did say that. I guess I'm not there yet." She flashes me an ornery grin that almost makes up for her being so mean. Almost. She clears her throat and drags one foot back and forth in front of her. "I um, I think it's nice you live with your mom. I'm assuming she lives alone. You haven't mentioned your father. I'm sure she likes having you so close. I have familial obligations as well. I promised my father I wouldn't give up the family secrets for profit." Her eyes plead with me to understand. "It was kind of his last wish." Her voice breaks.

"Your father's dying?"

She shakes her head while looking all confused. "No, that's not what I meant. I'm just saying that was like one of the last things he said to me when he moved to assisted living." She runs her hands over her face. "It's just the way he said it. Like I felt like he'd rather I lose the family farm before giving up our recipes." She wrings her hands. "I know it sounds crazy, but he made me promise."

"What if you donated the money you made to charity?"

She scrubs at the mixing bowl with a washcloth. "I just don't think I can. I promised my dad."

I don't know why I'm so set on this, but I've got a gut feeling about the landmine she's sitting on. "But if it was for charity, you wouldn't be making any money off it, so it's not the same thing as greed at all. Just think about it."

She gives me a look of exasperation. "You are exhausting."

I say nothing in return. I think the best thing to do is wait her out as she engages me in a staring contest, which if I'm not mistaken is getting to her by the way she fidgets.

"I don't know the first thing about patenting." She heads for the stove top. "Doesn't it like take a chunk of money to establish ownership of the product?"

"It does but I know the process pretty well. I've got a few friends who have done this sort of thing already. I helped them with it." I reach out and take the skillet from her to immerse it in the soapy water. "I could help you too. We could be like partners or whatever."

She nibbles on her lip. I want to too. "You've given me a lot to think about. This is a big decision. I don't know if I'm ready."

"I understand." I don't know why it's so important to me that she do what I'm asking her to do, but it is. "If it means anything, I believe in you. I think you could really make something happen with your family recipes. You just have to come up with a brand name and business logo or whatever."

"Why would you do this for me? We only just met this morning."

I turn to face her. "You're right, and I don't expect you to understand, but I believe there's a connection between us. I'm not ready to walk away from what could be."

"Even if I was hiding in that pantry at Tom's house?"

I can't believe I'm laughing. "I was pretty sure you were there." I hold her gaze. "I sensed your presence."

An awkward silence fills the space between us for too long. "Well, Tommy Jr. sure didn't. You should have seen his face when he opened the pantry door to find me sitting there on a bucket," she jokes. "You'd have thought he saw a ghost."

"What did you do?"

She looks a little sheepish. "What do you think I did? I looked at him like he was the intruder on my turf and walked on out of there as cool as you please." I believe her.

"You're one gutsy lady." I study her. "So have you ever been in love?"

She clears her throat. "That's a bit personal, don't you think."

"You don't have to answer."

She gets a silly grin on her face. My stomach sinks. She totally has. "Not with a human."

"What's that mean?" I can't even. She's cute, and sexy, and smart. But if she tells me she's in love with an anime character or some kind of *Star Trek* dude, I'm walking.

"I've had a few pets here and there. I love dogs and cats and horses." She says with a giggle. "I even had a pet hedgehog once."

"You fell in love with the prickliest animal there is. Now that I *can believe*."

Her eyes widen along with her grin. "Now who's being judgy?"

I can't help it. I chuckle. "This guy."

She nods. "Mm hmm." She leans back on the counter once more. She balances on the balls of her feet. "Have I ever loved a guy that wasn't family? No."

"What about Randy?" I truly hope she says no. Or laughs out loud.

She wrinkles her nose. "There is a difference between lust at first sight and love at first sight."

My ears perk up at the last four words. "So do you believe in love at first sight?" I can't believe how much I want her to.

She studies me as much as I study her. I think those hazel eyes of hers could be an X-ray machine. "My great-great-grandfather did."

I have no idea where this statement of hers is going. "And did it work out for him?"

She giggles. "Eventually. Do you want to hear the whole story?" I can't say no.

"Sure. I like a good story."

"I never met him of course, because he was my great-great-grandfather, but he lived to be 103 years old, and to answer your question, yes. He did marry her. They were married for seventy-six-and-a-half years."

"Wow. That's amazing," I say, because it is.

She smiles a small smile. "I think so. So the story passed down through the years is that he walked into a church and saw a little brown-eyed girl singing in the choir and that was it for him. He knew that day he was going to marry her."

"That's crazy."

"It's romantic."

"So they met and got married. End of story."

"Not quite. You see her brothers were wealthy and educated and they wanted her to go to college. They certainly didn't want her to marry a poor Kansas dirt farmer. But he was a stubborn man, if you can imagine that."

"I've met you, so yes, I can believe that."

"Thank you."

"That wasn't exactly a compliment."

She shrugs. "Mas or menos. So anyway, her brothers didn't want her to marry him. So she rejected his proposal."

"That's cold."

"Twice."

"Ouch."

"Yeah, but as I said, he was a stubborn man. So basically, he asked her one more time and told her that if she didn't say yes, he wasn't asking again."

"Ooh, he gave her an ultimatum."

"Yeah, and a bunch of sappy letters that my dad said just about made him vomit and they were definitely not worth reading." *I'm not sure why she's telling me that part of the story.*

"He must have been some love letter writer if she said yes."

She laughs out loud. "Actually, no. The rest of the story is that his sister was friends with this woman he was in love with, and it was his sister's letter to this woman who would become my great-great-grandmother that changed her mind. I guess his sister told her in the letter how miserable her brother had been ever since this woman turned him down twice and so that must have told his future wife how much he loved her."

"So his sister is the reason this woman accepted his marriage proposal."

She nods again. "Yep."

I twiddle my thumbs. "Well. I guess I'm out of luck. I don't have any sisters."

She giggles again. "Guess so. You're on your own." She looks me in the eye. "So to answer your question, no, I have never been in love. Not even close."

"I find it hard to believe no man has ever fallen for you."

"That's not what I said. I said I've never fallen in love with someone. I haven't dated all that much." She looks uneasy.

"Getting my degree and starting my own business kept me pretty busy. And then I had to move back home and get this farm going. There hasn't been anyone I'm willing to invest in. The other love of my life is books. We bookworms are not an easy lot to get close to. Half the time the love of our life is in a book. It's a lot easier to love a person who only exists between the pages."

"Yeah, 'cause they won't let you down."

"Um, duh."

"So, who's the love of your life between the pages?" I tease, but I really want to know.

She gets all quiet. "I don't know,"

I cross my arms on my chest. "Yes, you do. You don't have to tell me, but you totally know."

"Fine, but you're going to make fun of me and tell me it's generic."

"I won't." I hope I can keep a straight face. "So long as it's not Captain Jack Sparrow or Willy Wonka."

She pretends to think as she taps her finger on her chin. "Johnny Depp is dark and mysterious, but he's too pretty, and he's just so quirky, and I would never read either of those books."

I nod like I know what she's talking about. "Quirky is a bad thing. Noted." I wait for her to answer me, but she doesn't. "So who is it?"

"It's Mister Darcy."

"Ah." I make a mental note to google it as soon as possible.

"Don't tell me you've never watched *Pride & Prejudice!*"

"I saw the book cover for *Pride & Prejudice with Zombies.* My niece was reading it."

"That's the dumbest thing I've ever heard. I can't believe anyone would insult Jane Austen like that."

"Did you hear me say I didn't read it?"

"Yes. Sorry. I just can't even."

"You do realize it's all fiction."

"Yes, but he's so *tortured* by his love for her. That's what makes it so romantic."

"You find a man's suffering romantic?"

She smiles up at me. "What can I say? Mister Darcy makes suffering look so good." She raises her finger. "And I also like Brian Gilcrest in *Aloha*."

"And why is that? Is he also tortured in love?"

"Actually, yes he is, but that's not why I like him," she giggles.

"Why do you like him?"

"Because he's Bradley Cooper. Who doesn't like Bradley Cooper? He's just so good at being conflicted. Even when you can't stand his movie character you can't help but like some parts of him. He's just so charming."

"Is that your way of saying he's hot?"

She sticks her tiny nose in the air. "Don't ask questions you don't want answers to."

# ELEVEN
# BRIDGET

I RELIVE my entire day with Trevor Bennett as we stand here staring at each other. The man makes me absolutely crazy. I've never spilled my business to anyone like I just did with him and especially not in the first 24 hours. Is it because I've been so focused on work and school that the first person who comes along and acts like he cares about my life just opens the lid on everything I held in that I didn't know I wanted to come out?

My heart races inside my chest. *Holy crapola.* I think I'm having a panic attack. I've only had one once before and that was in my therapist's office the day I found out I had to move back home or my parents would be selling the family farm. And then I started to have one with the boar, but that's just because everyone was there at once and it was totally out of control. But I didn't. And I won't.

I so don't want to have a full-out panic attack in front of the first guy who has seriously turned my head. And my heart. *Shitake mushrooms.* I hate anxiety.

"Hey," he says. I'm already on the way to a meltdown.

"Yes." My chest heaves. My heartbeat pounds in my head. I can feel it. My throat is closing. I reach for a glass of water but my hand isn't agreeing with my brain as it knocks the glass of water to the floor.

His hand is on my throat. *What the heck is he doing?* "Your pulse is racing." His tone is Zen. I edge closer to hear better.

"Look at me," he says. "Can I breathe with you?" The usual amount of teasing is nowhere to be found. The sparkle and shine his eyes usually hold is gone. All I can see through my anxiety-induced haze is concern. I want to cry but I don't want to cry. Not in front of him.

"Breathe deep and hold it for as long as you can. One, two, three." He takes a deep breath and so do I. It's hard to focus but I hold it in as long as I can. I let it out and so does he. We do it again. I feel my heartbeat slowing down. This man is some sort of an emotion-managing magician. I think I'm in serious trouble. My heartbeat picks up at the thought. His hand remains on my neck. "Breathe in and hold it again." And so I do.

Many long minutes later, I feel somewhat normal. "I'm sorry." I feel like such an idiot.

His hand comes off my neck. He gives my arm a squeeze. "It's alright. You've had a big day. A wild boar died in your fields. I accused your neighbor of agroterrorism. You hid out in a pantry to spy on me. Which by the way is very flattering. You tried to teach me how to bake. We survived a miniature storm together and then your ex crashed your place all wet and weird." He lets out a big sigh. "And then I tried to force you to patent your family secrets." He pokes me gently in the arm. "Like I said, it's been a big day."

I nod. "I'm getting tired just hearing about it." I could leave it at that. I could let him believe that's what caused my anxiety but that would be a lie. "But that's not what brought it on."

"It's not?"

"Um, no. I've never… I've never been…" I stop, because I can't quite get it out.

"So attracted and connected to anyone ever before today?

Trust me, I know. I'm pretty hard to resist." Then his smile disappears. "Neither have I, Bridget, but there's something between us. I feel it. It's real. Unless you've got some dead body buried on your property that you're responsible for, I'm not going anywhere."

His words get to me. Big time. I choke a little. "Um, that's not what I was going to say. I was going to say that I've never opened up to anyone like I did with you today and that scares me," I admit. "And I've definitely never dumped all that on a complete stranger within twenty-four hours of meeting them." The look of rejection on his face is too much to take. "But to answer your question, no, I don't have any dead bodies on my property." I clear my throat. "That I'm aware of."

King Louie moseys into the kitchen and starts lapping the water I spilled off the floor.

"It's a good thing that was a plastic cup," Trevor muses as Louie gets it between his teeth and sets it up on the table. It makes Trevor laugh. "That's very clever." He congratulates Louie with a good ear scratching. "Good boy, King Louie."

I giggle. "My mother was OCD about cleaning. I think it rubbed off on him." I glance up at the clock on the kitchen wall. "It's past midnight." I blink. "How can it be past midnight? Where did the time go? Where are you staying?" There's only one place to stay in our small town and they generally close down at 10 p.m.

"I didn't plan that far ahead. Believe it or not I like to be spontaneous." Trevor looks me over one more time. "Besides, I had to see if you turned into some sort of strange-looking creature after midnight. I draw the line at hideous trolls with warts."

"You have a line for everything, don't you?"

"And you don't?"

I cross my arms on my chest. My head feels heavy. "It depends on the fairy tale. If you're talking about the greatest fairy tale of all time, the hour of transformation is sunrise."

"Is that your way of asking me to stay til morning? 'Cause I accept." The shock I just felt shows up on my face.

"In the guestroom, of course," he adds. "I can also sleep on the couch." He points to my living room. "I could keep King Louie company. I'm blanking on your sunrise reference though. I guess I need to brush up on my knowledge of fairy tales."

"Shrek and Fiona. It's got the best message. Gingy is my favorite. But Pinocchio slamming smooth-talking politicians, and their lying tongues is pretty good too. But that's in *Shrek 3*."

His eyes widen just a little. "Is there a soapbox you don't stand on?"

I shake my head back and forth. "In the words of John Cusack, 'Life is too short to not speak your truth.' Or something like that." My last words are much quieter. I ponder Trevor's inviting himself further into my life. It would be better for the both of us to have some distance between us, but it is rather late. It feels silly sending him down the road another forty-five miles just to find a place to sleep.

"You may stay in the guest bedroom, but Louie stays with me. All the bedrooms are upstairs. There's also a single bathroom. I will leave the light on. In the morning, you can shower in the basement. There's a makeshift showerhead down there in the corner. It's all cement flooring."

He appears to be listening, but his eyes are a little glazed over. "I'm guessing the shower is not in your room with the cauldron."

I give him a playful shove. "No, it is not." I glance around the room. This feels so strange. I feel like I should be more concerned about him staying over but it feels kind of nice. Maybe I'm lonelier than I thought I was. "Well, I guess we'll just head upstairs then." I walk in front of him. I feel his absence as soon as it happens.

"Just double checking the lock on your front door."

"Thanks."

He laughs. I turn back. He points at Louie who is sprawled out on the living room floor. "I don't think he's moving."

I can't help but smile even though my stomach is tied in knots. "I think you're right about that." I turn back around to hurry off to the bathroom and finish getting ready for bed. Fifteen minutes later, I emerge with my nightly ritual in place, a green tea facial mask. Trevor comes walking down in the hall in nothing but his boxer briefs, reminding me it's been way too long since I've been seriously attracted to anyone. I hope my eyes aren't bugging as I practically hug the opposite wall. I keep my eyes downcast while trying to get to my room at the end of the hall. Why did I think it was a good idea to have the guest bedroom catty-corner from mine?

"Good night." He totally knows what he's doing. Why is temptation so fun, and how am I going to get any sleep knowing we share the same hallway?

"Night." I duck into my room.

"Hey, Bridget. I'm sorry to bother you," *No you're not.* "But where do you keep your towels?" Trevor's yell is so loud that Louie lets out a low woof downstairs.

I pop my head out into the hallway and try to ignore the half of him I still see. "There should be clean towels in the bathroom cupboard. Just open one up and look."

"Right. Got it. I just don't like going through people's cupboards without their permission." He wears an apologetic grin, which I almost believe until I remember he invited himself to stay over.

"Feel free to snoop all you like. I'm not hiding anything."

His face falls a little. If he thinks I'm going to fall for his little plea for help, he's wrong. He's a grown man. He can find his own towel. "Alright. Well, thanks." He shuts the bathroom door.

I close my bedroom door and hop into bed. I open my laptop and get on Facebook to see if Karen or Alexia are still up. Alexia is. *Dang it.* I wanted it to be Karen. She's probably curled up and sound asleep beside her five cats.

I get on and message Alexia. "Hey, you got a minute?"

"Sure, what's up? Did you manage to get rid of Trevor? You gotta watch him. He's a smooth talker."

*Tell me about it.* "Actually, he's still here," I text and hit Send. Thank goodness we're not Facetiming. My walls are pretty thin.

"What? What are you doing with him?"

"It's been a long day. We got to talking, and he just stayed."

"So you're with him, with him. Like you two are a thing now?" She texts emoji bug eyes at me.

Not exactly. We kissed. He was pretty open with me about how he feels. His honesty is turning me inside out. I can't say any of that to her. Her emotions about Trevor seem pretty raw. "No. We aren't a thing. I invited him to supper. We cooked. We ate. We talked some more. It got late. I told him he could stay here."

"Trevor cooked for you." I think she's getting mad. Now I feel bad.

"We cooked together. He helped me cook."

"So you're FRIENDS now."

"We've been getting along alright. It wouldn't be the worst idea. I mean he's assessing my crops. I don't want to get into a fight with him." I feel stupid but I don't know what to say.

"Well, if he breaks your heart, don't say I didn't warn you."

They dated three years ago. She can really hold a grudge. I don't say that either. That would not be helpful.

"Thanks." I don't know what else to say. It wouldn't help for me to relay every time she's called me in tears after some guy she picked up at a bar slept over for two weeks in a row and then ghosted her. That's about how long it takes for something to make her mad. Then she flips out at him and then he's out the door. Reminding her would just come off as judgy. And she doesn't listen.

"Well, I guess I'll see how tomorrow goes."

"Yeah, I guess you will."

Oh, joy. I've just passed into the next phase of Alexia's anger. She starts parroting the person she's arguing with which is a good indication she's sirens-going-off irate. The girl has no filter.

"I'm gonna go now. It was nice talking to you."

"Yeah, you better go. Nice talking to you." She sends me a middle finger emoji.

"Okay, then. Love you too, Alexia," I say out loud as I close my laptop.

A knocking at the door makes me jump. "I'm out of the bathroom in case you want to wash that green tea off your face," Trevor says.

I climb out of bed as slow as a sloth and tiptoe across the room before turning the knob as quietly as possible and heading back to the bathroom. I close the door all the way and lock it. The scent of Trevor is everywhere. *What did the guy do? Spray a bottle of cologne in here?* I stare down at the faucet handles. It's so strange to think he touched them. Why am I thinking such ridiculous things? I duck my head over the sink as I rub at my face with a warm washcloth.

I stand here longer than usual as I let the warm water soak my skin. It feels so weird knowing he's right down the hall. I have no idea how I'm going to get any sleep tonight. Randy never stayed over now that I think of it. It wasn't for lack of trying. There were a few nights I came close to giving in but he lived right down the road. I couldn't put my finger on why I didn't let him but it just didn't feel right.

The thought hits me between the eyes. It doesn't bother me to have Trevor stay over, but it's different. Randy would have insisted on sleeping in my bed. That has to be it. I leave the bathroom light on and walk back down the hall. I climb into bed and close my eyes and hope for sleep to come. Tomorrow's only Tuesday.

Thoughts of the day catch up to me. I can't believe I kissed Trevor in the middle of the grocery store. In front of Randy and KayDee no less. Everyone knows she's the town's biggest gossip among other things. News of me making out in public with my crop inspector is the last thing I need going around town. I'm such an idiot. Why do I do these things?

I lay here on my pillow trying to settle down. "I will not be undone by one man," I whisper to myself. "And I will not feel guilty about kissing the crap out of him just to show Randy I'm over him. It's not my fault Randy was with the town gossip mill in aisle seven and now she has something to talk about. Besides, Trevor kissed me first so he's the one who started it. I am twenty-four years old and I'm responsible. I'm about to name my own business." I reach over to turn on white noise. I've got to get some sleep.

---

Morning comes before I know it. I slip a hoodie over my head and follow my nose to the kitchen. Trevor stands at my stove in one of my oversized tee shirts and a pair of my joggers that look more like yoga pants on him. He is so adorable. He turns in my direction. "Hope you don't mind me going through your drawers. I was trying to find something to wear to make you breakfast. I didn't think you'd be too happy with me if I wore just my boxers."

The image fills my head way too easily. I bonk my head on the doorframe I'm leaning in. "It's good you are wearing more clothes," I stumble over my words. "I wouldn't want you to get cold." His bedhead mussy hair is too much for my lonely heart to take. Dang it. I wasn't needy before he showed up. Now I'm already feeling his absence and he's still here. This is not good. I've never been a needy girl.

He waves a hand at the two coffee cups sitting on the

island. "I made you some coffee, but I don't know how you take it."

I cross the room and pick one up. I take a sip. That coffee could stand on its own. I grab the half-and-half from the fridge and pour as much as will fit in the coffee. I snag a pink artificial sweetener and dump that in too. "Thanks for the cup of coffee."

A honking outside makes me jump. Trevor looks confused as I rush towards the front door. Whoever it is, I don't want them seeing him in my house. I open the door before closing it behind me to step outside.

Sam Walsh stands at the bottom of my porch steps. He looks a little flustered. "Hey, there, Bridget. I was just coming by to remind you of the bike race that's happening today. You didn't answer my text last night. We rerouted the roads you know, because of the pig, so you'll actually be setting up your lemonade stand at Road P now."

"What time was that again?" I try to keep the Sheriff's focus but he's staring at something behind me. I'm pretty sure I know what.

"Sam," Trevor booms. "Good morning."

The Sheriff raises a hand in greeting at Trevor, but his eyes stare straight into mine. "Just read your text, Bridget," he says in a clipped voice.

"Got it. Will do."

I slip past Trevor to go back inside. "Must you be so boisterous?"

"I'm a morning person. I'm not going to apologize for it. Are you going to come into the kitchen and eat the breakfast I made you or what? And how much lemonade are we making for the cyclists?"

I stop walking. "You're going to help me make lemonade? Aren't you on a schedule?"

He shrugs. "I was, but this boar thing kind of put other things on hold." He waves his hands in the air. "I'm offering you two helping hands. Are you really going to turn me down?"

When he puts it that way, I feel silly saying no. "I guess not. How do you feel about making granola with me?"

"Give me a recipe, a bowl, and a spoon, and I'm your guy."

I sneak over to the stove to peek in the skillets. "You made eggs and sausage and hashbrowns. And they're the perfect shade of crispy."

He rushes up beside me smelling all kinds of yummy. His hair is still wet from the shower he must've taken in like a minute while I was talking to the Sheriff. I feel so grungy. He touches his bottom lip. "You got a little something right there."

I resist the urge to feel for it. I haven't eaten yet so it can't be food. "Oh, what's that?"

He leans in slowly. His eyes are stuck on my bottom lip. He's so hot. "Me," he whispers right before his lips touch mine. All I can do is smile. Trevor Bennett's kisses in the morning are the perfect way to wake up.

I grab the oven door handle and try to keep my head as he backs up and spins around to grab a plate. "So would you like some breakfast, or do I have to eat all that myself?" he asks innocently. I will my Jell-o knees to straighten up.

"I like breakfast."

"Go on and sit down," he orders. "I'll bring you your plate."

I don't know what to think. I've never had a guy make me breakfast or bring me anything. This is amazing.

## TWELVE
# TREVOR

I FEEL a little guilty for overwhelming Bridget by simply making her breakfast, but it's the least I can do after she put me up last night. I wish I could feel guilty for appreciating how she likes looking at me in my boxer briefs, but I just can't. It's nice to know she's not a robot. I was beginning to wonder. She's just so serious all the time about her farming. Work ethic isn't a bad thing, but if it makes someone immune to the basic laws of attraction, then they might have a problem.

From the appreciative look on her face, I'd say no guy has ever cooked her breakfast before and that's just sad. Then again, I've met Randy. He doesn't seem the type to know his way around a kitchen. I'd guess the only thing he knows how to crack is a beer tab.

I wince a little when I think of the work I'm neglecting. I've always been a guy who likes everything done a week ahead in advance, but that was before I met Bridget. I don't know what it is about her, but I want to stay here as long as I can. I enjoy her company. She's different from any woman I've ever met.

My phone goes off. It's Mac. I glance over at Bridget sipping her coffee. "I've got a work call. I'm just gonna step outside." I head for the door that leads to her backyard.

I skip reading his long text message and call his number. "Hello," he says in a confused voice, but that's fair. I rarely call him. I usually text.

"Hey. What's up?"

"Are you on the road yet?"

"Um, not exactly. I stayed the night for this boar thing."

There's an awkward pause on his end. I'm not sure what to make of it. "Did you stay at her house?"

"I did, but it's not what it sounds like." I glance up at her kitchen window to see if she's watching.

He laughs in my ear. "Oh, I'm sure it's exactly what it sounds like. I saw the way you were checking her out. I thought you understood after that last fiasco the level of professionalism expected between you and your clients. The boss is gonna fire your ass if he finds out about this. He warned you not to let it happen again."

I take a deep breath. "This time is different."

He chuckles. "Yeah, I've heard that one before too. That's what Mike says about every three months."

I kick the dirt. "What does Mike have to do with me? The guy's a total jerk. He has no sense of loyalty. He's always seeing at least two women at the same time. I can't believe you'd compare me to him." *Seriously.* I may have dated more than my share of women, but at least I date them one at a time.

"Yo, man. Chillax. I'm sorry, alright. How is this time different?" Mac asks.

"I don't know, man. She just is." I try to explain. "Like you *know me*, dude. I've *never* let a woman cut into my work schedule this much before even if these are extenuating circumstances. Ordinarily I'd just drive back through once we know the diagnosis for that boar. I wouldn't stay here waiting for the results. But something's going on."

"What do you mean? What's different?"

"It's different because I'm not just staying here 'cause I owe you a favor. I'm not just staying here so you won't have to drive back over here after the lab results come back. I'm here for her, and I'm not leaving until she knows. I gotta go. She's waiting on me to help her squeeze lemons for lemonade."

He laughs. "Is that guy code for something?"

I squirm a little at his teasing and insinuations. "No. I'm actually making lemonade to hand out to a bunch of men on bikes riding down dirt roads for recreation."

"What the hell? Why would you do that?"

"I told you. There's something about her." I feel a bit like an idiot. "Why else do you think I'd be sitting at a lemonade stand in the middle of a bunch of Iowa wheat fields?" I look up at the window. She's staring at me. *Crap.* "She's waiting on me. I gotta go," I hang up on him as he laughs. I suppose I should be offended, but I can't say that I blame him.

I jog across the yard and whip open the back door. She's already in the big bag of lemons lying on the counter. She squeezes the heck out of one over the cooler. By the look in her eye, I'd say it's a safe bet she wishes that lemon is my neck.

I pick up one and cut it in half as I venture another glance in her direction. "I can't believe we have to squeeze all these lemons into these coolers. It feels a bit ridiculous since it's for a bunch of bicyclists who I'm quite certain just want a drink of something cold."

"They'll need more than water to keep them going." Every word sounds like she takes a bite out of it.

"If you say so." I don't know why it's so much fun to fuel her fire.

"Everyone enjoys homemade lemonade. It's refreshing." She sounds as if she was eighty-five years old and wearing spectacles.

I step away to slice another lemon before squeezing the heck out of it over the cooler. "Whatever you say. You're the boss. If this is the way you want it done then I guess I'll have just have to do it your way."

My resignation earns me a steely-eyed glare. She blinks a

few times. I can tell another scathing remark is on the tip of her tongue. I brace myself for Round Three, I think. I don't know. I've lost track. All I know is trading insults with anyone else would send me packing, but Little Miss-Know-It-All hovering over her coolers with her lemons that are about as sour as her disposition is half the time has bewitched me.

"What time is it?" Her eyes fly to the clock on the wall. "Dang it. We need to get that granola in the oven." She gives the clock on the wall a second glance. "We've got to hurry. I'm doubling the recipe. So just measure everything times two." She points a juicy finger in the general direction of a bunch of stuff piled in the corner. I can't help but chuckle. She's awfully bossy for a little thing.

"Don't worry. I may just be a simple crop duster, but I think I can do basic math."

She tosses a big plastic bowl in the middle of the table. It almost falls off the side. I grab onto it as it flirts with going to the floor. "What's this for?"

"We need a bigger bowl if we're doubling it." She starts dumping things in there. "You measure the liquid and the granola. I'll get the rest."

I read the ingredients twice. "I've got everything but the maple syrup. Where is it?"

She points somewhere in the vicinity of six cupboards. "It's in there." I start opening doors. My eyes scan the multiple items stacked one on top of the other. I see no maple syrup. "Try down below."

"You're really not a morning person." I grin forgivingly at her.

"Not when I have less than an hour to make granola and lemonade for a bunch of bicyclists and I haven't had a decent cup of coffee."

"I'm sorry you don't like my coffee." My pride evaporates over her insulting my coffee.

"I'm sorry I don't either." She sounds sort of sorry.

"Aha. Maple syrup." I hold it up. "I don't know if we'll have enough."

"We'll have to make do. I'm not driving to the store now. Hurry up and stir it in. I've got to toss it in the oven."

Minutes later, she shoves a big flat stoneware pan in the oven. "Okay. I'm going to go shower. I'll be down ASAP and we can load up the Forerunner." She snaps her fingers. "You want to grab the card table and two chairs from the shed? We'll need them for our stand."

"You could say please and thank you."

She stops her little jog at the bottom stair. She's all limbs as she rushes me where I stand at the island. There may not be much to her, but I feel every bit of it when she jumps on me. I'm caught off guard and almost fall over while she's static cling. She kisses me a few times before running a hand through the top of my hair while she slides down the front of me and prances away. If I wasn't awake before, I am now. "W-w-what was that?" I think I was just assaulted but it felt wonderful.

She whips around with an ornery grin. "That was a please and thank you," she sings before jogging upstairs.

I fall back on a bar stool and try to find my balance. "Those are the nicest manners I've ever felt," I say to lazy Louie, who lays on the floor like a rug.

My phone dings. "Don't forget my table and chairs," I read.

"I'm on it," I answer as I walk towards the front door. It doesn't take me long to find the shed. I'm in the middle of opening the door when my cell phone rings. I cringe a little when I read Veronica Mayo's name. I really don't want to pick it up. We broke up six months ago, and she knows why. She's the only person I've ever known that made me regret mixing my business life with my personal life. I learned certain character traits about her that I never would want in an employee.

I thought our breakup was mostly amicable until she

stalked me via Instagram and Twitter for the next three months, making snide comments here and there every three days. Eventually the span between her online insults grew wider and wider until it finally dissipated. I was never so relieved, but I couldn't help but wonder who her next victim was. Her stalking wasn't enough to be considered full-on crazy but it was super annoying. Veronica is one of the three reasons I don't mind being on the road all the time. Karen and Alexia are the other two. I really struck out at dating my coworkers, which raises a hint of doubt about chasing after Bridget, but this is different. She's not my coworker, and I can't stay away.

I go to answer my phone, but it's already gone to voicemail. I hate that I'm OCD. It's going to bug me until I know what it's about. I'm pushing the voicemail button when my phone rings again. It's still Veronica. This must be important. I pick up.

"Hello," I say unenthusiastically. I have no idea how I'm supposed to answer the phone when the person I was practically inseparable from for two straight months calls. I dropped her because I caught her lifting one of my credit cards without asking. I shiver at the thought. It just felt so wrong. It was a terrible, awkward moment in so many ways. I shove that thought from my head. Mostly, as well as the urge to ask her if she obtained a new credit card in my name.

"Hey, Trevor," she says in a flirty voice. "How are you doing?"

*Cut the crap, Ronnie*, I want to say, but I don't because I don't want to turn what could be a ten-minute conversation into an hour while I wait for her to tell me what she's after, because the girl is always after something. "Veronica," I answer in a noncommittal voice. "What's up?"

"Funny you should ask, Trevor. You see, I need a really, really big favor."

I shove the groan that threatens to come out of me back

down. "I'm not giving you money. Our relationship was never like that."

"Because you wouldn't let it be."

"I don't even know how to answer that. Do you have a point, or did you call me up just to argue with me?" I blurt out because she's so annoying. "I'm *kind of* busy right now."

She sighs into the phone. I can't believe that noise ever turned me on. Veronica is a frequent sigher.

"I'm supposed to do a work presentation. It's my first webinar. I had someone all lined up. They bailed on me at the last minute. I could really use some support," she whines.

"Then why did you call me?"

"Because you owe me."

This girl is unbelievable and I'm about to tell her so.

"How do you figure that?" I all but yell. This shed is kind of echoey. I try to calm down. My voice doesn't sound so great bouncing all around. "I caught you red-handed."

"What are you talking about?" Either she has a terrible memory or she's really good at faking complete innocence.

"You took my card from my wallet without telling me."

She giggles. "Oh, yeah. That was you. My bad." She waits a long second. "So, anyway, about this webinar, could you help me or not?"

"What is the subject matter?" I can't believe I respond. She doesn't deserve any pity from me. She's a thief.

"I was going to have an epidemiologist talk about the latest disease concerns in our region."

"Which are?" I'm pretty sure she has no idea.

"They are whatever he was going to talk about before he up and quit and didn't bother to tell me."

"That sucks. There's no way you can get him to change his mind?"

"No. Trust me, I've tried. This webinar is in fourteen days. I have no idea how I'm supposed to wing it."

I shouldn't give her so much grief, but I can't believe she's sitting here telling me she can't B.S. her way through something. That's all she did when we were together. She liked to tell these crazy elaborate tales that I could never disprove but I just had this feeling they were embellished if there was any truth in them at all. "I'll think about it," I tell her.

I hear a sniffle. Oh, no. She can't be crying. I don't deal with crying women very well. "Trevor!" Bridget's scolding voice burns my ears. Her face pops in the doorway. Two long braids fall on her shoulders. Big bright flowers are all over her cloth overalls. Her light pink tennis shoes match her tee shirt. I never thought I could love pink so much.

"What's taking you so long?" she accuses.

"You can't think about it. I need to know now," Veronica insists through the phone.

"Okay, fine. I'll do it. Just don't get upset," I say in a calm voice because I don't know what else to do.

"I never said you had to do it," Bridget says in a quieter voice. She sounds hurt.

"What are you talking about?" I ask.

Her hazel eyes widen. She rocks back on her heels. "What are *you* talking about?" she fires back at me.

"Don't do it because you feel sorry for me." Veronica wails in my ear. I forgot how dramatic she can get. She's a total flip-flopper.

"I said I would do it, so I will. I need to go now," I bark.

"Fine," she says. "Shall we meet over dinner sometime soon and iron out all the details?" If I'm not mistaken, there's a breathiness to her tone. I think she's coming onto me.

"Then let's go, geez. You don't need to be rude," Bridget scolds. Talking to two women at the same time is very confusing.

"I'm not being rude and I'm not yelling. I was out here trying to do what you wanted done," I tell her in the most stress-free voice I can manage before turning away from her to end the call with Veronica.

"We've already talked about this. It's strictly work between us. That's all it can be. So accept my help and be grateful I'm still talking to you," I say before hanging up the phone. I turn back to Bridget. She looks like someone slapped her.

"Trust me. I've got it. You don't need to be so harsh. Geez," she says as she starts to walk away before whipping back around with fire in her eyes. "For the record, I never asked for your help, and I am *grateful*," she spits out the word.

I reach for her hand and grab a hold. "Hey. Look at me," I say and give her a little tug. "I was talking to a coworker, not you. I had a phone call."

"Was it a woman or a man?" she demands, even though I'm pretty sure she knows the answer.

I release the breath I was holding and proceed to dig my own grave. "It was a woman. She needs my help. She doesn't have anyone else. It's short notice. Someone canceled on her at the last minute." I don't know why I'm explaining work to Bridget. I don't owe her any answers. We kissed a few times. That doesn't make us anything special. She's so much as told me so. And it sucks.

She waves her hand at me in a swatting motion. "Sure. Okay. Whatever. It's not my concern anyway. I've just got to get all of this out to the site before cyclists come through. Sam says the first one will be there in about seven minutes so I gotta hustle."

Her eyes fly to the card table that I lay a hand on. Her whole body stiffens as she grabs a hold of the card table and tries to yank it out of my grasp. This shed just got a whole lot colder.

"Gimme my table."

I should let go. That would be the smart thing to do but she's being completely ridiculous. "No. Veronica is my coworker."

She snorts. "So, you're dating."

"We dated. We're not dating anymore."

"Does she know that?" She levels me with a look cold enough to freeze a whole lake before looking off somewhere else. She sniffs. She can't be crying too. This cannot be happening to me. I am not that horrible of a person.

Her question catches up to me. "Yeah. She knows that. Especially since it happened months ago. We haven't spoken much since."

I don't like the way she's looking all narrow-eyed at me like she doesn't believe a word I'm saying. "So she just called you out of the blue?"

"Yeah. Today was the first day I've heard from her in person since we broke up."

She taps her toe. "So you haven't heard from her since you ended things but your first instinct is to help her?"

I shrug. "I didn't want to, but she's desperate and she was upset."

"So she was begging. You made her beg."

For the life of me I do not understand females. "Are you upset with me because she was begging, because we broke up, because I talked to her, or because I agreed to help her with a work project? I'm pretty sure you're angry but I don't know why."

She makes a big show of looking at her watch. "Your business with Veronica is not my concern. Could you please hurry up and load the Forerunner? I'm going to be late, and I don't want to burn my granola."

I pfft. "How can you be late to a bicycle race? You're not getting paid to sit on the side of the road like an idiot, are you?"

She releases the card table, and it falls on my toe. I wince. "Oh, I'm sooo sorry," she sneers. "Did I drop something on you that you weren't expecting?" She runs out of the shed and back to the house.

I'm a human wrecking ball. I can't say anything right. I can't do anything right. I don't know why I try, but I can't seem to stop. My three trips between her Forerunner and the shed are rushed. I'm on my way to load a cooler when she snags the other handle.

"You don't have to help me. I can find someone else."

I'm sure she can and that's what rankles. "Is that what you want? You want Tommy Jr. to sit with you at your lemonade stand? I bet he'd be more than happy to keep you company. Maybe he'll bring you a few chickens to play with. Or how about the Sheriff? You could talk to each other on that two-way radio of his." I know I sound stupid, but she drives me completely insane.

"Just shut up and get in the passenger side. I'm driving."

# THIRTEEN
# BRIDGET

I CAN'T BELIEVE Trevor was standing out there in the shed talking to another girl after he just made me such a nice breakfast. What a two-timing snake. He was literally talking to her at the same time he was talking to me. He could have just told me he was on the phone and waited to talk to me instead of making me feel stupid. He'd better think twice before he tries to steal another kiss from me. I don't kiss liars.

My morning was going so well. Why did I have to walk in on his phone conversation? Why am I thinking like that? Do I really want him to lie to me about who else he's talking to? I will not be an ostrich with my head stuck in the sand, as my dad loved to say about anyone he thought ignored the truth staring them in the face.

Trevor said the phone call was work-related, but it felt like more than that. I don't know why I'm stressing about any of this. We aren't together. I don't want for us to be together. It would just complicate way too many things and that's the last thing I need right now.

I slam on the brakes right before backing into his Beamer parked behind my Forerunner. Trevor's eyes are wide open, but he doesn't say a word. I feel like a maniac as I drag it into drive and peel out of my own yard, creating lines in the grass.

"Veronica is a colleague," he starts up again. "She's supposed to be doing a webinar, but the person backed out on her. It was going to be with an epidemiologist."

"You're not an epidemiologist," I all but yell. "That's already been established. There is a big difference between an epidemiologist and someone who assesses crops."

Trevor's hand flies to the bill of his hat which he moves up and down. Just watching him go through the motions makes me itchy. I don't know why guys are always messing with their hats. He turns to look at me and the sunlight catches his eyes once more. Darn that sun and the way it lights up his baby blues. They look like the Mediterranean. I want to dip my toe in...or something. His pearly whites flash at me. "What you lookin' at?" he teases, like he already knows how devastating he is to my senses.

I jerk my head back around. It's a wonder I'm not in the ditch. The man is too distracting. "I'm watchin' the road," I bark.

"Hmm mmm," he all but purrs. "That must be why you just missed your turn." He points at my rearview mirror. I blush in embarrassment at the three cars that just turned behind me.

"What the heck," I mutter while looking for a good place to flip a U-ey. "Does it really take eight people to run one lemonade stand?"

"Slow down and take that turn-in right there," he instructs while pointing at the road in front of us. "Slow down."

I slam on the brakes. I can't take his nagging.

"You keep doin' that and you're gonna spill the dang lemonade and then we'll have to go back to the house and make more," he roars at me. We sit in the middle of a country road halfway up or down a hill, which is just about how my life feels right now.

"I was supposed to be married at 23," I mutter to myself as I creep towards the turn-in before backing out onto the road.

"What's marriage got to do with anything?" Trevor asks. His voice is all croaky.

I put my Forerunner in drive and start back towards the road I missed. "Nothin'. I was just thinking about roads I missed or ones I haven't taken yet, and I thought I would have by now," I get out while kicking myself because I want to cry. This is just stupid. The man has already made my eyes water too many times. I don't need this kind of headache in my life. I am not an emotional person.

He squirms in his seat. "Well. I don't know if anyone's ever told you or not, but life's not a race and some things can't be rushed. I mean, heck, anyone can get married. It's whether or not you meet the right person that counts," he reasons, and it sounds rational but I'm not having the best morning.

"Of course you say that. You're a guy. All you men worry about is how fast some girl's going to tie you down. Y'all like to act like marriage and children make up some great imposition and we women are just out to get you any way we can." I know I'm not being fair, but still.

He sniffs. "You *are* out to get us. The last girl I broke up with tried to steal from me. I caught her red-handed."

"What'd she do? Ask you to pay for dinner?" I'm not sure I'm being fair. He hasn't done anything yet to make me think he's the type of guy who would ask a lady to pay for him.

He shakes his head in the seat beside me. "You know what? Forget it. Let's just agree to not talk for a while. You're not going to listen to anything I have to say. You're too busy making me the bad guy when I didn't do anything to deserve it."

*Yeah, right. We had a wonderful breakfast together and you ruined it by talking to another woman on the phone right after. I should have trusted my instincts. You're a major player.*

"Fine by me," I answer just as we pull up to the spot

marked by cones. I hop out of the Forerunner and head around to the back to unload. The table is a little awkward, but I manage to get it out along with the chairs. I get all the food arranged along with the cups and coolers of ice. All that is left are the big coolers with the lemonade and water in them. They're too heavy for me to carry. Trevor knows this. He's just waiting for me to ask for his help. He can wait all day long as far as I'm concerned.

I busy myself with divvying up rations of granola into sandwich bags. A cyclist is coming. I glance at Trevor, who stares at me from the passenger side. I can't believe he's being such a stubborn jackass. I point towards the road and throw up my hands. He just keeps staring. "Would you like lemonade or water?" I yell at the man.

"Water," he replies. I grab a cup off the table and make a mad dash to the back of the Forerunner for the cooler that sits a ways back. Hauling myself up in the back is no easy task. Neither is sliding the heavy cooler across the Forerunner bed. I lean over the side and somehow push the button down while holding the cup underneath, silently cursing Trevor all the while. He's the reason I feel like a crazy fool while I straddle the cooler and hope I don't lose my balance and take a header off the back of my Forerunner.

"There's granola on the table," I get out as the first rider eyes the men coming up behind him on their bikes.

I scooch the other cooler up as far as it will move before hopping to the ground to run for more cups. I restrain myself from flipping the bird at Trevor on the way back to the coolers. "Water or lemonade?" I ask as I gasp for breath.

"Why aren't these coolers at the table?" a grandpa barks at me.

"I can't lift them," I growl back at him.

"How'd you get them in there?"

*Get on your bike and ride away, Grandpa, and leave me to my worries.* I smile politely and ask one more time. "Would you like water or lemonade?"

He takes a hose-looking thing off the top of his hat and takes a long draw. "I don't need any hydration. I've got my own," he says with a grin before situating himself back on his bicycle and riding away.

I turn to the person next in line. "Water or lemonade?" This forced politeness is going to kill me before today is done.

The man hops off his bike and puts the kickstand down. He's built like a mountain. "I can grab those coolers for ya, mate," he offers. Oh, yummy. He's Australian. I'm a sucker for accents. He grabs a cooler and lowers it to the ground with a half squat. Holy cannoli! He made that look so easy.

I grab a hold of the one side and try not to check him out as we walk along. "Thanks for sitting out here on a Saturday for us thirsty bikers," he says with a flirty grin. "You beauty."

*I'd sit out here all day for someone like you*, I think. I think I thought. I hope I thought. I watch his face for any recognition of my thirsty statement. Did he just call me beautiful? "Sure," I answer. "That's no problem."

His hand brushes mine as he grabs both sides of the cooler. "I've got this," he says with a slight grunt as he lifts it onto the table. "Let's go for the other one, mate."

I follow him back. Trevor steps out from behind the Forerunner carrying the other cooler. It's a bit wonky. I can tell he's struggling. His face is a little pink from the exertion, but he keeps going. The bicyclist slaps Trevor on the back a little too hard and he almost falls down. If it was intentional, that was a dirty trick. "Thanks, mate. There for a minute, I thought you were a real bludger," the Aussie says with a wicked grin.

Trevor's answer is to say nothing in return and keep walking.

"Thanks again," I tell the Australian. "I guess you better keep riding."

"Yeah, I will. I came over here with a mate. He wanted to do the race. I think I left him behind," he says as he puffs out his chest. He looks over at me. His green eyes soften. His shaggy blonde hair falls over one eyebrow. He's so tan and so fit. "You got any ankle biters?"

"Yes. I've got one. He's a bump on a log. His bark is worse than his bite though."

He looks confused. "One child, then? That makes sense. You seem like a clucky sheila."

I'm not sure what he's talking about but he's a real hottie and he's smiling at me. I nod about the time his words catch up to me. "I don't have a child. I have a dog."

He claps his hands. "Crikey, I'm a dag," he exclaims. "Would you like to have some brekky with me tomorrow before I take off then?"

"I'm sorry," I reply. I'm not following.

We're back at his bike. "Food. In the morning," he replies, but he sounds a little irritated. "Would you like to eat with me?"

I consider Trevor for all of half a second. He was just talking to another girl this morning, so why does it matter what he thinks? I've never had a date with an Australian. I pause. Is it a date? It's breakfast. *Don't overthink it.* He's already riding away. "I'd love to," I holler after him.

He looks back. His back tire wobbles. "Come find me after the race," he answers. I can't help but smile at his salmon shorts and the crabs on his cream-colored shirt.

"Gotta date lined up, do ya?" Trevor growls from the passenger seat of my Forerunner as I walk by.

"Looks like it. You gonna sit in the car all day?"

"Yep."

I skip over to the table with a smile. "I'm having breakfast with an Aussie," I say mostly to myself before sitting down and ignoring Trevor glaring at me through the windshield.

Mostly. The steady flow of bicyclists helps me ignore Trevor's blatant staring.

I look up at the college-aged girl straddling her bicycle. "Lemonade or water?" I ask with a friendly smile.

# FOURTEEN
# TREVOR

I CAN'T BELIEVE the nerve of this woman. She just picked up a breakfast date for tomorrow in the middle of handing out lemonade to bicyclists with a muscle man from Australia. Right in front of me. It's complete lunacy. Where does she think that relationship is going to go, and what is she doing with him? I thought we had the start of something. Our chemistry is off the charts.

I know one thing. I certainly don't need to be sitting here feeling like a complete idiot when she's over there making plans with another guy. She clearly doesn't want to be with me. I'm not about to beg for her attention. There are so many other things I could be doing or places I could be off to for my job. I stare out the windshield at Bridget as she serves the bicyclists their drinks and hands them some granola. She's the reason I can't leave. I want to be where she is. All the time. This is becoming a real problem.

I summon the courage of my father and grandfather who both met their future wives when they were engaged to other men. I know it's not the same, but still. Watching Bridget blatantly check out Mister tan surfer-man, with his pearly-white smile and all his muscles, was all I could take. My stomach hurts just thinking about it. I'm not out to win any beauty contests but I felt relatively confident about my looks until he showed up. The sexy accent was bad enough. He didn't have to break out the big guns by hauling her cooler over to the table in his ridiculous excuse for a shirt and second-skin spandex. I wasn't about to let him do it twice. I squeezed all the lemons that went in that homemade lemonade, not him.

All he did was show up on his little bicycle and look all buff while carrying a cooler eight feet. That's not that impressive. I open the door of the Forerunner. I may not be charming, but I can get under her skin.

"Did you make a decision about that patent?" I call. There's no one at the table waiting for a drink.

She shoves the chair next to her over a few more feet. I ignore the slight before walking around the table to plop down in it. "Thanks. I don't know if I can take any more steps. My feet are tired of walking," I say all dramatically.

Her arms cross on her chest. She looks off in the other direction. "Wouldn't it be a conflict of interest to have a stake in a company that sells fertilizer, since you're a crop assessor and all?" She doesn't sound too worried about it.

Crapola. I hadn't thought of that. "It shouldn't be. So long as I'm not actively trying to sell your product exclusively to farmers when I do my assessments."

"And you've done a lot of this sort of thing?" Her hazel eyes look me over as if to check if I'm lying.

"More than you. Have you ever written paperwork for a patent?"

She shakes her head back and forth. "No, I haven't, but that's because I have zero interest in doing so."

I tap my fingers on the table. "I have a friend who could look over everything once it's done. Just to be sure everything is kosher and there's no confusion about where the funds will go for any money made."

"To charity," she confirms in a straight-forward manner. "It will be going to charity."

"To charity."

"And you'll back me financially."

"I will."

"No questions asked and no arguing over ideas because this is my baby."

I nod as I raise my hands. "Discussions will be held about pricing product and marketing and advertising costs, but ultimately any business decisions will be made by you."

She leans back in her chair. "I need to see it in writing. I need to see a proposal, a projected outcome, as well as a projected timeline for the release of the product; everything. I want to know what I'm getting into."

I'm stuck for half a second on her facial expression. She's so serious and so driven. It's so sexy. I've never been so attracted to someone in my life. By the excited look on her face about the experiment, I'd say she has no idea how gorgeous she is. I nod while trying to find speech. "Of course. I'll get the paperwork started as soon as possible," I answer. "Do you have a brand name or logo yet?"

She groans a little. "I'm still workin' on that."

I knock on the table. "Well, I've got an idea for a good distraction. Veronica needs a subject for her Webinar and we just tested that pig for glanders. Even if it tests negative, we can still talk about the possibility of glanders and what precautions would need to be taken. All of that stuff needs to be covered, and this seems like a good opportunity to raise awareness for critical situations related to disease."

"He probably doesn't even have glanders. It feels like you are making a mountain out of a molehill." She sounds on the verge of hysterics.

I wonder why that is. It can't be all due to the pig, can it? "If he had glanders, wouldn't you want to know?"

She shrugs. "I don't know. It was just one pig." She waves

her hands around. "You've got the *entire* county blocked off for no good reason. No one is transporting any animals anywhere. It won't be long, and the local newspaper and the Chamber of Commerce will have everyone up in arms. You just wait and see. The yearly rodeo event isn't far off. This county better not be on lockdown when that time comes. You'll have people lined up for a city block protesting the quarantine. You don't interrupt the yearly rodeo event for something that *might be* an issue."

I've had about enough of her warnings. "You listen here, missy. I'm just trying to follow the guidelines I've been given by the state of Iowa. I'm not about to lose my job because doing it pisses off a bunch of rodeo cowboys. If they can't bring their horses or cows in here because of possible exposure to a deadly contagious virus, they'll just have to deal with it and cut their losses. This has the potential to be a grave situation."

She snorts in derision. "Groundbreaking? Really? A boar keels over and dies and it's international news. Don't be absurd."

My phone vibrates. I glance at the name. It's Mac. I can't believe the level of excitement I feel. "Whatta you got?" I ask in an expectant tone.

"Relax, Trev. You know it takes a little bit to isolate the bacteria from the skin lesions. We can't very well detect an antibody response to the bacteria in a dead boar. But it should be quicker than it normally would be because I sent it to Canada. Their turnaround time is phenomenal." I wish I had his confidence. He has no idea the venomous stare-down I'm getting from Bridget at this exact moment. I think she wants my head on a stick.

"How much is that going to cost the state?" I demand.

"Chill out. In cases like these, they make exceptions. Believe it or not, labs are willing to take on some if not all of the costs when something out of the ordinary happens. They'll probably make this into like a whole case study they use to train students in handling Tier 1 agents. This is heavy. I can't believe it turned up in Iowa. That's why they consider it a bioterrorism threat."

Bridget's eyes widen. "There's no way that Tommy Jr. could have done this on purpose. He's not that calculating. I'm telling you it was an honest mistake on his part to import such a sick animal." She stares at my phone that is on speaker. "How long is the incubation period?" she asks Mac.

He clears his throat. "Although it's not clearly definitive, it is most likely to be spread between animals between one to fourteen days after exposure, but most animals get it within five days of exposure. But there's also evidence that shows it could be from six days to many months, so it's just hard to say."

She groans. "There is no way in the world you're going to tell the entire community they might have to quarantine their animals for longer than a week. You'll be lucky if you can get them to last that long."

Awkward silence follows. "Would it help for community members to know the mortality rate in humans if they get glanders, or the fact that it's highly contagious, or the fact that they don't want it going through their livestock? If it got into a herd of cows, the results could be disastrous," Mac points out.

Bridget closes her eyes and tilts her head back to stare up at the sky with her eyes closed. "This is so exhausting. We don't even know if the boar has the glanders."

I clear my throat. "I know that. But it could be. And if it is, it would be extremely careless and irresponsible of us to just treat this as a 'wait and see' type of ordeal. I am acting in the interests of the entire county and its livestock when I say there has to be a county-wide lockdown in place for all transport of livestock and any other animal until we know for certain the threat of the spread of whatever illness that boar has is gone."

Bridget groans. "Okay, fine. I get it. You two are like a

broken record. I swear. Can we please talk about something other than glanders and contagion? You're giving me a headache."

"Later guys," Mac says. I barely hear him as I end the call. My focus is on the highly annoyed woman staring out at the fields. Her entire face appears flushed. Every muscle in her body is tense. She wasn't kidding about being stressed.

"Want to talk about your secret recipes?"

She sighs. "Not really."

"How about your date with the Australian?"

She looks in my direction. "Not with you, I don't. All you'll do is point out every flaw he might have." She rubs her fingertip on her forehead repeatedly in a circular motion. "I don't want to hear it. It's just breakfast."

I raise an eyebrow. "Maybe, but maybe his idea of breakfast starts the night before. Maybe he wants a sleepover." My stomach feels as hard as a rock. I didn't think I was such a fan of self-torture. I glance down the dirt road. We haven't seen a bicyclist for the last fifteen minutes. I look at the cups in the trash and the ones on the table. "I don't suppose you kept count of how many cyclists have gone by?"

She rolls her eyes at me. "Yeah, I had them all sign a guest book while they were waiting for their crumpets and tea."

"Are you always this friendly?" I try but I don't know why. She seems determined to be a rain cloud.

She frowns. She jerks sideways in her lawn chair so suddenly she almost flips it sideways, but her pink Converse catch her just in time. She opens her mouth. I can only imagine what's going to come flying out of it. One hand rests firmly on her hip. She grips the material of her overalls so tight her knuckles are white. She makes a goofy face with her lips while slowly closing them. I think she just bit her inner cheek. Slowly but surely, she turns away from me and slinks into a slouch in the back of her chair. Her arms cross on her chest, a familiar action. "I'm sorry."

That was anticlimactic to say the least. Her eyes close. Her pink nail taps on her arm. The bright shiny nail looks out of place next to the rest of her farmgirl look. I guess she wasn't joking when she said she was once a city girl. "It's been a long couple of days, but that's not your fault. Well, most of it isn't your fault."

What? "How is *any of this* my fault? I didn't ask you to go chasing after the first muscle head that comes along and asks you to breakfast. You just got done sending ding-dong Randy in his soaking wet tee shirt away and now this one shows up." I know I sound pathetic, but I can't help it. The line of guys waiting to date her is a bit much. She's not the only one who's had some crappy days.

Her finger that had been on pause is back to circling, but now it's both hands and they've moved onto her temples from what I can see. She leans forward in her chair, bent over at the waist. "The guys aren't part of my long week."

I'm officially an idiot. "Of course." I slap my leg in frustration. "They would be part of *my* long week."

Her hand drops on my knee. She gives me a squeeze. I feel zinged up to my hairline. "I said I was sorry." She looks up at me. "Besides you never know who might have connections to marking and advertising."

I sniff. "Do you really think Randy or Mr. Muscles is going to help you sell your product?"

She leans back in her chair. Dang it. Her hand is no longer on my knee. "I don't know. It might." She nudges my foot with hers. "I don't know why you're being all pouty about my social calendar, mister Ag ho. I don't think I'll be taking you to any agricultural meetings anytime soon. Or maybe I should. You could probably find me a few sugar mommas to sponsor our product. It would save me a lot of marketing and advertising."

I shift in my chair. "I am not a piece of meat."

She gives me the once-over. Her hazel eyes light up for the

first time this morning. I'm not sure I like it. "I wouldn't be too sure about that." She glances at her watch. "I'm giving it ten more minutes and then I'm calling it."

Sam's Sheriff truck peeks over the hill. He slows down to a creep. I note the moment he sees me. His beaming smile for Bridget loses a little luster as it slowly flattens out. "Morning," he says with a wave of his finger as he speeds up and keeps on going. I give him a wave.

Bridget waves wildly. "Hey, Sam." She starts towards his truck but stops when he shows no signs of slowing. She turns to me. "What's his problem?"

I stare at her like she's clueless, because *honestly*. "I have no idea."

# FIFTEEN
# BRIDGET

TREVOR ACTING like some lovesick schoolboy is a little flattering, but mostly it's annoying because it messes with my concentration. That is exactly what I don't need when I'm trying to think up a logo and brand-name for being a sell-out. Why am I doing this? Every time I think of giving up my family secrets, I want to puke. It's just ever since Trevor mentioned that their secrets die with me, I've felt extremely selfish about not sharing them. It's not that fair that he knows me well enough to figure out challenging me is the easiest way to get me going. My family secrets will sell because they work. I know that for a fact. It's not about me. It's about the hard work my parents, grandparents, and their ancestors passed down to future generations. They didn't intend to leave a legacy. They wanted to pass on foolproof instructions written in black and white to get the next generation through hard times.

And I guess it doesn't matter if my fertilizer hasn't had enough time to be officially tested or whatever. As long as I don't sell it with some sort of guarantee, I can't be held liable if it doesn't churn out the crop. I am only responsible for the product I sell, not the way someone chooses to use it. I wish I knew the line between justification and obligation. Why did all of this information end up in my lap? Why couldn't I have had a sibling to fight me on this? Why am I blaming my parents for not having more children? This is all madness.

I suppose it might sound cheesy to some, but whenever I stand in my mother's kitchen rolling out dough and slicing apples, I imagine her doing the same thing when she was my age. I have to wonder if her mother studied her with the same smile on her face that my mother gave to me - a smile that said, "Well done." Her look of approval felt as warm as a hug.

"Hard times," I say out loud to see how it feels as we load the table in the Forerunner.

"Excuse me?" Trevor asks, but he's distracted.

"Hard times."

"What's that?" He's paying attention this time.

I stare out at the field and recall the first year I was back and the countless nights I spent at my kitchen window praying the weather would cooperate with my testing trials for the fertilizer I was developing. Every inch of skin on the palm of my hands bore callouses from the days I spent digging and planting. I thought I'd go cross-eyed labeling each row according to the mixture of fertilizer I had tweaked this way and that trying to get it just right.

The moment I picked up that 4x6 index card containing the base of my fertilizer, I knew it was my destiny. I'd never felt such strong ties to my family until I stumbled upon it. That was the moment I knew the farm my dad left me was more than just a piece of land or a headache.

When I read the contents of the fertilizer, I felt like an idea was imprinted in my brain. I had a chance to make a difference in the world of agriculture. It wasn't my pride that told me I was the right person for the job. It was just something that I knew.

I wouldn't have believed my story if someone else had told me that they didn't know how they knew. They just did. I remember words and measurements flying into my head as I read over the card scrawled by past generations. It was like I couldn't rewrite them fast enough. I'd taken plenty of Ag classes in college, but I've never had a photographic memory. The final recipe for the fertilizer I use that has proven to be true time and time again is nothing short of divine intervention. I have no other way to explain it. The more I think about it, the more I realize Trevor is right. It would be a shame for me to not share it with others.

"What are you thinking about?" Trevor asks as we pull up to the end of the race.

I look over at him. "My secrets." I smile before hopping out. I'm so confused. "Why are you driving my Forerunner?"

He shrugs. "You were pretty distracted. I asked if I could and you didn't say no." He gives me a wink. "You've been staring out the passenger side window for the last fifteen minutes."

My face heats. "I'm really sorry. I had something on my mind." I climb out of the Forerunner.

His friendly grin dims. "Hopefully it's not him." He looks at me across the top roof of my car before walking away.

I turn around to see who he's looking at and I'm lifted off my feet. Someone's lips are on mine, and they're not very gentle. *Gross.* That's way too much saliva and sweat. I back away. "Hey," I say to the Aussie who has me wrapped up in a bear hug.

"I got fifth place," he declares. I think he just spit on me again. I resist the urge to wipe it off, but it's all too much. I duck down while grabbing at my shirt, tugging it out of my overalls, and wiping my face on it.

"That's great. Congratulations."

He lets me go slowly, but not without making sure I slide down his front. He's very excited. It's a bit much, just like his monstrous hand that covers half my neck and shoulder at the same time. "So you ready to go then?" His hand floats down the side of me, tracing every curve along the way. It's so invasive. I'm officially creeped out.

"Where are we going?" I force myself not to run in the other direction.

His hand grabs onto mine long enough to pull me in, but then it's roaming again. I've never been one for public PDA, especially with someone I met less than an hour ago. *Unless it's Trevor. Darn the man. I can't get him out of my mind.*

Aussie tugs on me, forcing me back to the present. He's either slow on the uptake or he's completely unaware of my uncomfortableness. "Let's go. I've got the room until tomorrow. That oughtta give us time for a

few tosses before breakfast."

My jaw drops. His grin grows. He really doesn't do subtle. Or not so subtle. "Thanks, but no thanks. I think I'll stay here."

His look of confusion is priceless. He's either never been turned down or he's really good at faking it. "You don't want to go with me."

I nod. "That's right."

"But we were getting along so well. You're a wonderful kisser."

I close my mouth so I don't say anything rude. He's a terrible kisser. "I'm sorry. I didn't know." I try to sound sorrier than I feel. I've never been mauled so blatantly where there wasn't alcohol involved, and this guy just did it twice in such a short time. I don't care how hot this guy is, he doesn't have my permission to frisk me. He wedges his thick finger through my overall loop and gives me a tug. I bump into him. His hand is in my hair. This guy doesn't give up. I shove him a little harder. He's like a statue. I almost fall over backwards as the force of my shove hits me. The Aussie's smile grows. What the heck is going on?

"You're playing hard to get."

This is unbelievable. What else do I have to do to get him to go? I take a few steps backwards. "That's so not what I'm doing." He's beyond hearing anything I've got to say. He's like a dog with a squeaky toy, and I'm the toy. I glance around. How did we get sequestered into this shady corner, and why do I feel hunted? His friendly smile is gone. He's either constipated or just focusing really hard. Neither option makes me feel better than the other.

His hand is out in front of him. "There, there," he whispers at me as if I'm a scared animal, which is what I feel like right about now as my back bumps into the wall of the building behind me. "Don't be scared. I won't hurt you."

"I don't know how you pick up girls in Australia, but this sort of thing isn't done here." I've never been one to be afraid. I hate myself for it.

He stops moving. He blinks a few times as if he just woke up. He takes another step towards me but stops with a scowl. "Forget it, you're not worth it. There's plenty of other women I could eat breakfast with." If he thinks that's going to work on me, he's crazy.

I wave at him as if to shoo him away. I'm barely holding it together. "That's a great idea," I get out in a breathless voice. He stalks away with all his hunkiness. I'm such an idiot. I can't believe I didn't see what Trevor saw all along. The guy is a predator. I lean sideways into the wall and focus on breathing while my chest heaves. I'm shaking all over. I know he couldn't have done much because it's daylight, but the thought of meeting him in the dark gets me shaking all over again. I'd like to think he would hear me if I refused him, but he was a little too slow on the uptake. I'm still not sure when he intended to stop.

"Bridget."

My eyes fly open at the sound of Sheriff Sam's voice. I take a deep breath and try to gather myself before turning to look him in the eye.

"Sam," I say, but then I fall apart. The thought of the Australian running his hands over me like he owned me assails me all at once. I feel like I'm trying to hug the wall, but I'm just trying to get away from it all. When Sam's hand touches my upper arm, I fall into him. I need a hug. I need my father.

Sam holds me tight. It feels just right as I snuggle into his warmth. "There, there." I can't help but notice he sounds completely different than the deranged Aussie backing me into the corner. I start crying all over again.

"I'm sorry. There was a guy and he scared me," I get out in between hiccups and sobs. I can't believe I'm falling apart like this. I never fall apart.

"Was it Trevor?" he growls.

I shake my head. "No. He would never," I bury my wet face into his uniform. My response was automatic but, deep down, I know it's true. Trevor would never do anything to hurt me. Neither would Sam, and it's probably for the same reason. I feel bad that I don't feel anything for Sam, not in the way he would like. My feelings for Trevor are different and far from professional. I push those thoughts away.

Sam pats the back of my head awkwardly. "Hey, now. You're alright. Bridget. Get a hold of yourself, now."

Something in his voice makes me straighten up. I take the inside of my shirt collar and wipe my face to dry it. I'm so embarrassed. I can hardly look him in the eye. "I'm sorry, Sam. I don't know what came over me."

He looks off to the side and shrugs. "That's alright. We all have our days." His crow's feet wrinkle when he looks at me once more. "Maybe your tears will bring on the rain. We could really use some more moisture."

I sniffle as I nod. "You're right about that. It's a little too dry for the middle of June." I dig the toe of my shoe in the dirt. "This lack of rain has really tested my fertilizer this year."

He taps an antsy finger on his holster. "You gonna be alright then?" He tries to sound like it's no big deal, but I hear his concern.

I clear my throat. "Yeah, Sam. I'm fine. Thanks." I manage to look him in the eye and give him a smile. I take a deep breath. "I suppose we all fall apart now and then but I hate when it's me," I answer with quivering lips.

He throws his arm around my shoulders and gives me a squeeze. "Chin up, Bridget. You are your father's daughter."

I shove my hands in my pockets and take another deep breath or two before smiling up at him. "Thanks, Sam. That's just what I needed."

"Anytime," he assures me before making crazy eyes at me, cracking me up. Sam is always good for a laugh.

## SIXTEEN
# TREVOR

JUST ABOUT THE time I think I'll never find Bridget in the middle of all the bicyclists I hear her telling laughter. I mosey around the corner in her direction with a grin on my face but come up short when I spy her attached at the hip to Sheriff Sam. He's so busy making moony eyes at her he doesn't notice me approaching.

"Howdy," I say to the two of them.

Bridget takes her sweet time breaking eye contact with the Sheriff whose arm remains around her as they start towards me. "Hey, Trevor," she says. "What are you doing?"

Sheriff Sam eyeballs me with interest too, but it doesn't feel the same as hers. "Yeah, don't you have things to do? Shouldn't you be on the road by now?" he asks.

I shake my head. "Nah. I'm still waiting on the results of that dead boar," I say. "Besides, Bridget and I are working together on a project."

She frowns at me like I said something I shouldn't. *What's that about*? I thought she and the Sheriff were best friends. His arm falls from her shoulder. Finally. He tips his hat like in an old-time movie. What the heck? This isn't the old West. We're in Iowa, not Montana.

"Bridget," he says before walking past me just close enough to make me think he might bump into me, but he doesn't. I resist the urge to lean away from him when his steady eyes meets mine. We're around the same height. It feels like I'm in super slow motion as we stare each other down. I'll be danged if I look away first.

Bridget's hand on my arm has my head turning towards her and away from the space the Sheriff just occupied. "My nerves are shot. Do you mind taking me h-h-home?"

I nod. I can't believe how much I wish we shared a place together.

"Hey, Bridget," the Aussie hollers out from across the street, "Don't worry about tomorrow."

I turn back to see her face, but she's glued to my back. Her hand bunches my shirt and her head rests against me. I don't know what to think. "Are you that upset that you can't look at him?" I hate that I'm upset about it still, but I think I know now why she wants to go home. She's feeling rejected by Surfer boy.

"Can we just leave? I don't want to be here."

"Fine. Sure. Let's go."

"Where'd you park?" She hasn't let go of the back of me but I feel her peeking around me a few times. *What is going on?*

I point down the street in the direction the Aussie is walking. "It's just a few blocks down."

She peeks out around me for the third time. "Can we walk down the back alley until we get there? I don't want to be anywhere near him."

She's being a bit ridiculous about being rejected but if she wants to stay out of his sight that's fine by me. "Alright. But you're probably going to see three times as many cats. They like those back alleys."

She giggles. "I'm not allergic." She links her arm with mine. "Are you allergic?"

"Not that I know of." I remember the Sheriff when I come

around the corner. They seemed like they'd been there for a little while. "What were you doing with the Sheriff?" I ask.

She almost trips over her own two feet as we walk down the alleyway. "We were just talking." That doesn't sit well with me.

"About what?"

"Not much."

It feels like she's being deliberately vague. I wonder why. "You were talking about something. Obviously, you don't want to tell me."

She says nothing in return. It's maddening. I know I'm right. "Just like you don't want to tell me about why the Aussie isn't having breakfast with you."

Her lip quivers.

"This is ridiculous. You hardly knew the guy. If you ask me, he didn't seem like someone who knew important people, Bridget. You don't need his connections. There will be plenty of others," I encourage.

She nods and looks off in the other direction. Her hand flies to her face. She's crying. I can't believe she's crying over not getting to eat breakfast with the stupid Aussie. He wasn't *that special*. I wonder if she'd get that upset about me. I feel terrible for thinking these things. I wish I could stop. Bridget says nothing as we walk down the alley. The tension builds with every step we take. She's as tense as she can be by the time we get to the car. I don't know what to do or what to think but I know one thing. I'm not spending a whole afternoon watching her sulk over some other guy, no matter how cool his accent is.

I take the keys and hand them to her as we stand by her car. "Are you sure you want me to come back to the house? You don't seem like you're up for company."

Bridget's too busy scanning the street to look at me. I know who she's searching for. The golden tan man. Just about the time I think I'll get no answer, she speaks. "I already told you

I'd like you to come back to the house with me. Is that alright with you?" She's yet to look at me.

"I don't think he's out here."

"Can you just unlock the car?" Her jaw is tight. She almost looks nervous. I hit the key fob button and she's in the car with the door closed. Could I have read her wrong? Is she scared? Why would she be scared?

I climb in her car and start it up. She locks the door and puts on her sunglasses. My hand goes to the back of her seat as I back out into the road. I can't help but notice the farther out of town we get the more she relaxes. Maybe it wasn't about the Aussie. "You gonna tell me what's up?"

She says nothing. She just turns and stares out the window for the longest time. We're almost to the house. I decide to just wait her out and not worry about whatever is eating at her. "You were right about him."

"Who?" I'm lost in my own thoughts.

"The Aussie."

"Okay." I'm still at a loss. I have no idea what I was right about.

"He's a total tool." There's something more than agreement in her voice. There's fear.

"What happened?"

Her hands tremble in her lap. "It's nothing. I just got scared. I'm probably overly sensitive is all." She shrinks into herself.

Rage fills me like I've never felt before. He obviously did something to scare her and it wasn't nothing. "What happened?"

"I met him where Sam and I were when you found us." She stares off in the other direction. "At first he just picked me up off the ground and kissed me, and that was okay." It doesn't sound like she was very excited about his kiss. That makes me feel pretty good. "But then he put me down, and he just, I don't know…"

"What? What did he do?"

Her hands fidget in her lap. "He held me up against him so tight. I didn't like it. And then when I tried to get him to slow down, he just kept putting his hands on me like he had the right... and I didn't like it."

Rage fills me. I want to explode. I feel like I need to hit something. "Is that all?"

"Well, he wanted me to go with him to his room, like right then. I said I wasn't up for that, and that's when he started backing me into the corner like he was corralling a horse or something. He just kept trying to shush me or calm me, but he wouldn't stop coming at me. He was just so big."

"How did you get him to stop?" I'm not sure I want to know.

"I just kept telling him 'no', but he ignored me. So I spoke louder, and then he finally heard me. He left me alone and that's when Sam found me. I was still shaking so, and so he held me." She turns to me with tears in her eyes. Her hands are still trembling. "I'm sorry, Trevor. I don't usually fall apart like this. The guy just got to me." Tears run down her cheeks. I want to wipe them away, but after what she just went through, I don't know if she wants me to touch her. "I didn't mind Sam being there, but I wanted my dad. Or you. I guess Australia is not as nice as I thought he was. He's probably not used to being told no either."

"That's no reason to not accept it!"

She shakes her head. "Of course not. I didn't mean he should do what he did because someone rejected him. I'm just saying."

I want to pound the guy's face in. "I'm sorry that happened to you." There's nothing I can say to make any of it better.

She stares out the window again. "Yeah, well. I guess if that's the closest I come to being a victim I should consider myself fortunate."

I'm not sure I agree but I'm relieved nothing more

happened and that he showed his true colors before he got her in a room all alone. My skin crawls just thinking about it. We pull up the driveway. Bridget's front porch is covered with potted mums of every color imaginable. I turn to look at her. She's still staring out her window. "You've got some flowers on your porch."

She turns to look. Her eyes widen just about the time her mouth opens. "What in the world?" She climbs out of the Beamer, heads for her porch, and shakes her head as she walks in between the pots. She turns to look at me with questions in her eyes.

# SEVENTEEN
# BRIDGET

I CAN HARDLY BELIEVE my eyes. I have no idea how all these potted mums got on my porch. It surely wasn't Trevor. By the look on his face, he's as clueless as I am. It couldn't have been the weirdo Australian. He was already walking with another unsuspecting victim when we drove away. And it can't be Tommy Jr. He's too cheap to buy all these flowers. That only leaves Randy, but why would he do this?

These thoughts assail me as I meet Trevor's skeptical eye, but he also wears a smirk. "I see I've got competition."

My face heats like it always does when he starts up his flirtatious ways. "I don't know who—"

He snorts. "I do. It's gotta be Randy. He thinks I'm honing in on you, and he's upped his game." I feel so strange. I've never had two guys fighting over me, or whatever this is called.

"Don't go accusing me of encouraging him."

Trevor doesn't say anything as he walks in my direction. I can't help but notice he's got a little swagger going on. I should find his cockiness annoying but it's adorable. His blue-grey eyes are stuck on me, and I don't mind a bit. "Am I?" His low, quiet voice makes my pulse all jumpy.

"Are you what?"

"Honing in on you." He gives me a small smile as his hand touches mine.

Heat hits me everywhere. I can't think when he stands this close. All I see is his lips moving. I want them to stop. I want them on mine. I don't know what I want. "Do you want to be?"

His eyes darken the longer he holds my gaze. It feels like forever. I don't know why he won't say something. His thumb tracing shapes on the back of my hand says something, that's for darn sure. It tells me I'm in trouble because I've finally met a man I can't resist, and he's my crop assessor/soon-to-be business partner. None of this is a good idea, and I'll remember that tomorrow when I'm not standing in front of him waiting to be kissed.

"All I know is the longer I'm with you, the harder it is to walk away. I've never minded driving alone or the many hours spent on the highway, but now that I've met you, I feel like I'm looking for something every time I leave you." He stomps his foot on the ground. "So I guess what I'm saying is the place I need to be is here. With you. For as long as you'll have me." He eyes the potted mums scattered all around. "Between the bicyclist, Tommy Jr., and your ex- boyfriend sending you flowers, I'm a little worried who else will show up next. I'd better stick around just in case."

I give him a small smile. I appreciate his attempt at humor to lighten the declaration of devotion he just dropped on my front porch. It's so unexpected. We've only just met, but somehow it also makes sense. I take his hand in mine, giving it a squeeze as I look him in the eye. "Come on in, then. The house feels empty without you." I step on tiptoe to peck him on the lips. "And don't worry about those other guys, it'll take more than a dying boar to keep me away from you."

His eyes widen in surprise. He tips his head back and

laughs out loud before looking me in the eyes once more. He chuckles as he draws my hand to his lips. "You're definitely the girl for me. I should have known I'd meet the girl of my dreams in the fields..."

"Where love grows." I finish his sentence.

He nods decisively. "In fields where love grows." He tilts his head. "That kind of has a ring to it."

I shake my head, turn away, and open my front door. "In fields where love grows? That's the business logo you want? What's the rest of it? Bell-Bennett-BAM!"

He claps his hands behind me. "Yes, that's exactly it. That should totally be our business name. Bell-Bennett-BAM. In fields where love grows. That's the *perfect* name for a fertilizer."

I don't stop until I get to the kitchen. "I don't know. I think I can make it better." I measure coffee grounds to start another pot. "Besides, it's not just for fertilizer. It's also for the family recipe for apple pie, the cleaner, and our canned peach preserves." Something tells me it's going to be a long afternoon.

His arms wrap me up about the time I sense his presence. His chin rests on the top of my head as we sway back and forth. "You're overthinking it, Bridget. Don't. There's nothing wrong with simple. All of those things can be called BAM."

"BAM."

His chin digs in just a little. "Yeah, like BAM, this peach jelly is the bomb. Or BAM, that apple pie hits the spot. Or BAM, look at my plants grow!"

My giggles start and don't stop. I'm bent over at the waist. I'm laughing so hard. He releases me on my way to the floor. I cling to the counter for stability. When I finally get a hold of myself, I turn around. His hip juts into the counter that he leans against. He looks all calm and cool. My feet follow my line of sight as I take a few steps in his direction.

"BAM," I say all sweet and low, with the same amount of awe I just heard from him, "you sure look good holding up my counter." I close the gap between us and rest against his chest. He's all warm and inviting and just the right amount of soap and spice. I hear his heartbeat. It races along with mine. "How could I not know I was waiting for you all this time?"

His hands are on my hips. His fingertips dig in. I love every second of it. "I don't know, but you found me, and that's all that matters."

"BAM right, I did."

He laughs out loud. "See! I told you it would grow on you. You kind of like it, don't you?"

"It's getting there," I say with a giggle that comes straight from my heart. I tuck a finger in his collar and lean back just a little to look him in the eye, even though he's tugging on me, drawing me in. "*You've* grown on me. I think it's fair to say we could have the right stuff to produce a fine and healthy crop that withstands whatever trials come our way, perseveres in hard times, and has just the right amount of sustainability."

His face fills with confusion. "Are you talking about farming or a future generation?"

I gaze up at him. "I don't know, but it sounds like a pretty good family motto to me." I stand on tiptoe, lean in, and hover over his lips. "You decide." I settle in for a long kiss. Satisfaction fills me when I feel his knees buckle just before he hugs me tighter than I thought imaginable. His lips leave mine. They travel along my jaw, closer to my ear.

"If this is how you win, darlin', I don't mind arguin'."

I giggle despite the fact I'm burning a little hotter with every kiss. "I wasn't arguin'."

He breathes softly in my ear, sending me through the roof. "If that was some sort of proposal, I accept."

My heart sings with joy. It wasn't what I was asking for necessarily, but the words just spilled out before I could think to stop them. "Okay."

"Okay."

We both take a deep breath. I slowly get back to flat feet again, though I hardly feel it. My head is still in the clouds as I rest my cheek on his chest.

"BAM," we utter softly at the same time.

Don't miss out on your next favorite book!

Join the Satin Romance mailing list
www.satinromance.com/mail.html

————

**THANK YOU FOR READING**

————

Did you enjoy this book?

We invite you to leave a review at your favorite book site, such
as Goodreads, Amazon, Barnes & Noble, etc.

**DID YOU KNOW THAT LEAVING A REVIEW…**

- Helps other readers find books they may enjoy.
- Gives you a chance to let your voice be heard.
- Gives authors recognition for their hard work.
- Doesn't have to be long. A sentence or two about
  why you liked the book will do.

# ABOUT THE AUTHOR

I live in the beautiful Flint Hills of Kansas. I'm blessed to do two things I love- nursing and writing. I have wonderful family support including my husband, our son, daughter-in-law, and two daughters, my parents and in-laws, and too many more to mention as well as many friends who willingly give their input whenever it is requested. I'm thankful for the characters and stories as they come along, as well as the companies who publish them and readers who read them.

facebook.com/RachelAnneJonesAuthor

x.com/Jones1974Ra

instagram.com/diari197

tiktok.com/@idreamofdandelions

# ALSO BY RACHEL ANNE JONES

**With Satin Romance**

*A Joy-Filled Christmas*

*Pickles-N-Fries and Fireflies*

*Stealing the Glass Slipper*

*A Stolen Heart*

*The Last Living Beauty Queen*

*In Fields Where Love Grows*

**With Fire & Ice YA Books**

**_Novels_**

*Marmalade Uncapped*

*Essence of Emma*

*Lovestruck: Kisses, Lies & Oatmeal Cream Pies*

**_All Or Nothing Series_**

*Chasing Denver*

*Rough Terrain*

*A Firm Plateau*

**Radioactive Series**

*Love and Armageddon*

*House of Cinders*

*M.I.A.*

*The X-Factor*